Paweł Huelle was born in 1957. The author of *Who Was David Weiser?*, Huelle is a novelist, playwright and journalist who has lived most of his life in Gdańsk. His latest novel *Castorp* was published in Poland in 2004.

Mercedes-Benz

from *Letters to Hrabal*

Paweł Huelle

Translated by Antonia Lloyd-Jones

The right of Paweł Huelle to be identified as the author
of this work has been asserted by him in accordance with
the Copyright, Designs and Patents Act 1988

Published by Społeczny Instytut Wydawniczy Znak in 2002
in Krakow, Poland

First published in this English translation in 2005 by
Serpent's Tail, 4 Blackstock Mews, London N4 2BT
website: www.serpentstail.com

Designed and typeset by Sue Lamble
Printed by Mackays of Chatham, plc

1 2 3 4 5 6 7 8 9 10

F/00248957.

'This is the way you are going
even before your heart fell silent'

Józef Czechowicz, *Elegy of Sorrow*

Education and Culture

Culture 2000   With the support of the Culture 2000
                programme of the European Union

Grateful thanks to Faber and Faber Ltd for permission to
quote from *The Waste Land* by T.S.Eliot.

Milý pane Bohušku, a tak zase život udělal mimořádnou smyčku –
My dear Mr Hrabal, once again life has turned an extraordinary circle, for as I remember that evening in May, when for the first time I sat in a state of terror behind the wheel of Miss Ciwle's tiny Fiat – the only lady instructor at the Corrado driving school ("We guarantee a driving licence for the lowest price in town"), the only woman among all those self-important males: ex-rally drivers and racetrack aces; once I had fastened my seatbelt and positioned the rear-view mirror according to her instructions, to move off seconds later up the narrow little street in first gear merely to stop again, forty metres on, at the crossroads where only a narrow stream of air, like an invisible flight corridor, ran between the trams and the thundering trucks over to the other side of the city-centre inferno; as I set off on that very first car journey of mine, feeling that the whole idea of learning to drive made no sense at all, because it was too late in life, and I'd already missed the moment; when right in the middle of the crossroads between the No. 13 tram, bells clanging as it braked suddenly, and a

great big transporter truck, which by some miracle managed
to miss the little Fiat by a hair's breadth, while sounding its
awfully deep, shrill horn like a battleship siren; when I stalled
at the very centre of that crossroads, I immediately thought of
you and those charming motorcycling lessons of yours, when
on your 250cc Java motorbike, with the instructor behind and
the wet cobblestones ahead, you stepped on the gas and
sashayed off down those Prague streets and crossroads, first
up the hill towards Hradčany, then down towards the Vltava,
and the whole time, without ever stopping, as if inspired by
the Muse of Motorisation, you told the instructor about those
wonderful vehicles of bygone days, on which your stepfather
had so many fantastic crashes and smashes. So when the truck
driver brought his ten-ton monster to a sudden halt and,
leaving it in the middle of the road, jumped down from the cab
and ran towards Miss Ciwle's little Fiat, waving his fist at us
in a threatening manner, and indeed, in his rage coming close
to self-harm by pummelling his own head with it; when I saw
his face, purple with fury and pain, pressed to the window of
Miss Ciwle's little Fiat, and then another face right beside it,
belonging to the driver of the No. 13 tram, who like the truck
driver had abandoned his vehicle and his passengers, sent
flying by the sharp braking; when I saw those two faces
through the Fiat windows – which with great foresight Miss
Ciwle had already wound up – with yet more looming up
behind them, because the drivers of other cars blocked by the
tram and the truck had also left their vehicles and run up to us

now, to shower us in all their anger about traffic jams, broken bridges, rising petrol prices and everything else affecting them since the recent collapse of communism; when these Bosch-like faces had all but crushed us into the seats of the little car, which was adamantly refusing to start, I turned to Miss Ciwle and in a perfectly calm tone of voice I said: "You know, when my grandmother Maria was learning to drive in a Citroën in 1925, she had a similar experience, except that the Citroën stalled on a railway crossing, and from the right, where the instructor, Mr Czarzasty, was sitting, the Wilno–Baranowicze–Lwów express was fast approaching from round the corner when he made a rapid assessment of the situation and said: 'Miss Maria, let's jump out immediately or we'll be killed.' So they jumped out," I went on, "and the express, although it braked, showers of sparks flying from under its wheels, completely flattened the beautiful car. So there they stood by the field crossing: Grandmother Maria and her instructor, watching the engine driver's eyes grow bigger and bigger as in this whole pile of tin, nickel, chrome, plush, leather and broken glass he failed to find any crushed heads, chopped-off legs or driver's caps – not even a single drop of blood; only when he looked a little harder did he notice them giving him a friendly wave, and a very fine scene it was," I said, reaching the finale, "because right behind them by that field road stood the chapel of Our Lady of Perpetual Succour, with a ring of village women and children round it, right in the middle of May Mass. So the foreground scene of the crushed car and the puffing locomotive gently gave way to the middle distance, i.e. the driver clutching his temples, while behind him Grandmother Maria and Mr Czarzasty stood happily filling in the background – all set against the undulating hills at the foot of the Eastern Carpathians."

"Goodness, how beautiful," said Miss Ciwle, neatly sliding herself across into the driver's seat over my knees, while I deftly performed a similar movement in the opposite direction beneath her. "God, how well you tell a story," she went on, checking the gears and the ignition. "But why doesn't it work in my dual control either? Hmmm, I wonder…" She finally got the engine started and, showing our entourage of drivers that most mannish and indecent of signs with her middle finger, she slowly advanced along the human avenue, masterfully weaving her way among the throng of our would-be tormentors, eager to flog us on the spot at that dreadful crossroads, that first car-driving Calvary of mine.

So then of course, when Miss Ciwle said in that strange, slightly metallic voice of hers: "God, how well you tell a story," I already had it on the tip of my tongue to say "I'm nothing – you'd far better read Hrabal's *Evening Driving Lesson* – there you'll find the sort of stories every instructor should think about before falling asleep, or before taking a student out into town, there you'll find some real poetry in mechanised motion, a full exposition of the Platonic idea that the relationship between instructor and student doesn't rely on simple instruction or commonplace teaching, but on telling each other beautiful stories, on the sort of verbal communion that brings people together over and above gender, politics and origin" – but unfortunately, Mr Hrabal, I didn't say it, because my eyes were out on stalks, my heart was fluttering in my throat, and my tongue was as dry as if I'd spent three days at a Kashubian wedding when I saw Miss Ciwle suddenly step on the gas and slalom between those rabid drivers, parting the crowd with the square nose of the Fiat, and then, at literally the final second, leaping across the narrow gorge between the moving tram and the slowly advancing truck. Oh, what a pity you couldn't see that, dear Mr Hrabal – the victory of a young woman in a tiny Fiat over a crowd of yelling drivers and over those two awful macho men: the driver of the No. 13 tram and the truck driver, who, to make no bones about it, quite simply went crazy at the sight of the little Fiat crossing right in front of their noses, that hazardous leap between the Scylla of the tram and the Charybdis of the truck. Oh, Mr Hrabal, it was truly magnificent, that triumph of intellect over the masses, that ironical dig at senseless exasperation, as Miss Ciwle and her student cocked a snook at them: chin chin and up yours, you silly old fools.

"Jesus Christ," I gasped, "how well you drive! I'm devastated." "Why so?" she said, with a ringing laugh. "Because I'll never be such a master of the art," I said, gulping, "I'll never reach your standard, no matter what." "Now now," she said, "I've seen guys like you before, still waters, right?" And fixing her grey eyes on me she said: "But please finish

your story about your grandmother, I mean about the crushed
Citroën and the damaged train. Was the car insured, and did
the instructor get some sort of compensation? The damage to
the train must have been the railway company's problem,
surely?" She glanced at me again, with a look that was even
stranger than her weird name. "Well no, actually," I replied,
"it was quite different from what you think. In those days the
cars usually belonged to the clients themselves, to the
students, I meant to say, while the instructors hired
themselves out, like dance teachers or piano tuners. At the
agreed hour Mr Czarzasty would ride up to the client's house
on his bicycle, release his trouser leg from its safety pin, which
incidentally was a silver souvenir pin with a little diamond
stud that he immediately pinned to his English tie, then
straighten his peaked cap and sometimes his shirt cuffs too
before heading for the appointed doorway or garden gate,
checking his watch to see if he was a minute before time, in
which case he walked slowly, because in those days it was very
bad to be late, but even worse to be early. So, to get to the
point, the Citroën belonged to my grandmother Maria, who
got it as a present from my grandfather Karol, who at that
time was still her fiancé and was finishing his specialist
studies in Berlin. As my grandmother had forgotten to insure
the car, Mr Czarzasty got very upset at the level crossing that
day, for how was she going to tell her fiancé about it? Maybe
better to send a letter, but under no circumstances a telegram,
advised the instructor, because telegrams always bring bad

news and in this case the result would certainly be a breaking of the engagement, and Engineer Karol was such a good fellow, he said. Meanwhile, once the remains of the car had been pushed off the tracks, the engine driver carefully inspected his locomotive; first the buffers, then the lamps, and finally he looked under the front wheels and felt the pistons, but he couldn't find any trace of the impact – there were no cracks, not even a minor scratch, which put him in a state of despair, for which of his managers would believe that such a big delay was caused by ramming a French car? Who would take his word for it when there were no marks on the train? Even if the conductors or someone important from among the passengers bore witness, they'd still know better, they'd still cut his bonus or even worse, demote him to a lower category of driver, and never again – at this point he was almost in tears – would he drive the express from Wilno to Lwów or the Lwów–Warsaw–Poznań–Berlin sleeper, but fortunately..."

We had stopped at a red light, and I could tell Miss Ciwle was really enjoying my story, because she'd completely forgotten that it was I who should be at the wheel. "But fortunately," I went on, "travelling in the first-class carriage of that train was Mr Henry Robinson, a reporter for the London *Times* who had been sent to Eastern Małopolska to gather material on the Hucuł highlanders. So this Robinson was the first person to jump down from the carriage and had set to work at once. 'That's terrific,' he muttered, as he photographed the carcass of the French car. 'Just like Waterloo,' he kept saying contentedly, aiming his lens at the Citroën emblem lying in the mud. 'Quite remarkable,' he chuckled, snapping the Polish locomotive, which he later compared in his article to a Slavonic Wellington. Yes, and just imagine, thanks to those photographs and the piece in *The Times*, the engine driver didn't get a reprimand for being late, but quite the opposite – he got a gold watch and a reward, while a few days later Grandmother Maria, in spite of the fact that her Citroën, as I've already said, was not insured, was given the keys to a brand new car by Mr Rosset himself, Citroën's director for the whole of Eastern Europe." "I don't believe it!" cried Miss Ciwle, glancing in the mirror. "A gold watch and a new Citroën? A car like that must have cost a fortune, probably even more than nowadays." "That's right," I said, "but it was all thanks to the Anglo-Saxon press, which had great power in those days. Because if, for instance, just anyone had put those pictures of the squashed Citroën and the unscratched Polish locomotive in, let's say, the *Lwów Courier*, or the *Eastern Małopolska Dispatch*, if just anyone had written about it, which in fact they did in the *Illustrated Daily Courier*, even if they'd included photos straight from the scene, not even a simple child would have believed it. 'There's as much truth here,' they'd have snapped, 'as in a fairy tale. How can you believe it?' they'd gaggle. 'As if the locomotive wasn't even scratched, and how can you believe the luck of those two people who managed to jump out of the car in time?

Oh, we've come across this sort of *chutzpah* before – it's nonsense to imagine the young lady and her instructor were saved by Our Lady. How dare they mix religion with sensation in our country, or, even worse, with advertising!' But when the matter saw the light of day a few days later in *The Times*, well, the reactions were completely different. First of all Mr Willman Cox from London called the managing director of the engine factory at Chrzanów and said: 'My dear Mr Zieliński, we'd like to order fifteen locomotives from your factory. That's just for starters – between ourselves, I can tell you in confidence, ever since I've been in charge of British Railways I've never known anything like it! Ordinary people keep calling me up and shouting down the telephone, why don't we have locomotives like that? Why in the motherland of Watt and Stephenson aren't we making little gems like that one? We insist our trains be served by these very engines and no others. But that's not the end of it,' he gushed. 'My dear Mr Zieliński, can you just imagine, Sir, that yesterday I received a telephone call from Downing Street? The Prime Minister's personal secretary was good enough to inform me that the picture of your locomotive, which had disembowelled that French monstrosity, that Republican sardine tin of theirs, afforded the Prime Minister and the Prince of Wales the greatest satisfaction, prompting his Highness to condescend to ask the Prime Minister a question about our balance of trade with your heroic country, upon which the Minister of Communications approached me about your factory, whereupon I replied that I have been in contact with you for a long time, but that my hands are tied by our tariffs on steam engines, semaphores *et cetera*; to which the Minister said that can be arranged at a session of the House of Commons. So, my dear Sir, I hasten to inform you that we are placing an official order for fifteen engines, without any trial runs, and if you would like to entrust the intermediation to us – I realise it is always a delicate matter – we can sell twenty engines for you to Australia, thirty-two to India, seven to Ceylon, eight to Bantustan and one to the Falkland Islands, just one, because we are only now planning the first railway line there.' "

"Please stop, I beg you," said Miss Ciwle, raising her hands from the steering wheel. "Please stop or we'll smash into the kerb. What about the Citroën?" she promptly asked, indicating right and moving slowly across the tram lines into the turning lane, "what about the new Citroën?" "First there's the watch," I said, feeling the critical moment approaching, "the engine driver's gold Omega! So just imagine, immediately after that call from Mr Cox to the director of the Chrzanów engine factory a rumour went round that the driver should be decorated. 'How can such a deserving person be left unrewarded? It could only happen in our country, where what counts are favouritism and indulgence, not honest hard work.' So when the order came via Warsaw to the Lwów railway board, they immediately tried to summon him from his route by telegraph, but it turned out that on that critical day engine driver Hnatiuk had taken the two-weeks' overdue leave owing to him and had vanished into thin air. And he'd have been left in peace if it weren't for all the phone calls – first from the Warsaw railway board, then from the Ministry of Communications, then of Industry, and finally of Internal Affairs. 'Where's that valiant engine driver?' they kept shouting down the line. 'He's done more for us than a dozen commercial attachés,' they cried. 'Why can't the people in Lwów find out where the devil he's spending his holiday? We're a strategic national company! In the Poznań district it would be Inconceivable – with a capital I! It looks as if it's high time for some changes in Eastern Małopolska, because plainly everyone is thinking in national terms these days except for our colleagues in Lwów – maybe you don't even know the war has ended, gentlemen, maybe you still have portraits of Franz Joseph in his coronation uniform hanging in your office, maybe on your station clocks time is at a standstill, in so far as you have any idea what time means for our Polish economy!' These were no longer just threats," I told Miss Ciwle, who had just stopped the car between some striped rubber posts. "They were the harbingers of revolution, and as you probably know, revolutions were never a Galician speciality – apart from the one when the peasants reduced the manor houses to ashes and butchered their masters with saws, ever so slowly and methodically, for all those years of indigence and servitude... Yes, there was nothing they were more afraid of in that fine city than harbingers of change, because changes have a typical habit of turning good into

worse, and worse into really bad. That's what they reckoned in
Lwów and thereabouts, at least during the last fifty years of
the Austro-Hungarian Monarchy, so not just the railway staff
were mobilised, but also the secret agents, the police consta-
bles, officers and inspectors – all in vain, because at the little
cottage in Zamarstynów, where amid apple trees, sweet and
sour cherries, bean poles, corn stalks, sprouting hops and
grapevines engine driver Hnatiuk lived with his wife and two
children, there was no trace of him. 'Lord above, gen'lemen,
'ow on earth can I 'elp you?' said Mrs Hnatiuk, wringing her
hands. "E's not on duty, and I'd be glad to know myself what's
become of 'im, the rascal, I'd give 'im a drubbing myself, but
well, what do you know: 'e came 'ome and said "It's the end",
took two 'undred zlotys and that's the last we saw of 'im, and
it's a disaster cos 'e 'ardly ever drinks at all, but to deal with a
worry like that 'e's sure to 'ave spent the 'ole lot on vodka and
sausage and gone into the mountains, like in 'is bachelor days
– 'e always did like tramping about the back roads on 'is own,
so go and look for 'im, maybe 'e's at the pub in Kołomyja, or
Kuty.' At this point Officer Lamparski frowned angrily and
interrupted: 'Mrs Hnatiuk, are you trying to tell us that you
don't know where your own husband has gone on holiday?
Are you being serious? Don't you understand there's no time
to lose? This is a matter of national importance!' White as a
sheet, the engine driver's wife sat on a chair and gasped: 'Lord
above, gen'lemen, 'e's got nothing to do with any politics,
none of them banned papers, 'e steers clear of the

communists, so what's all this about?' Suddenly raising her head and her voice she proudly continued: "E's done nothing criminal, 'e turns up at work on time, so what the 'ell are you after 'ere in our 'ome?' "

Though amused, Miss Ciwle finally came to the actual point of our lesson. "All right then, please take the driver's seat," she said, getting out of the car. "First the mirrors, then your seatbelt, good, now let's start up and do the slalom!" Why did she choose the most difficult task of all for my first steering exercise? I'll never know. Maybe she wanted to put me in my place for being such a show-off, who instead of performing instructions properly gets out of it by telling stories from half a century ago; then again maybe that's not what she was thinking at all. But the fact is I was sweating like a pig, my hands wouldn't stop shaking, and I knocked over enough rubber posts to win me the title of world champion, if only they'd been skittles. My dear Mr Hrabal, you can't begin to imagine what it's like driving a good forty metres in reverse gear down a narrow track as curved as an ellipse, falling out of orbit once in a while, or knocking over a post and stalling the engine. After all, those evening lessons of yours on the Java motorbike, as you and your instructor, Mr Fořztík, swished your way through Vinohrady or Žižkov, as golden maple leaves dropped poetically into the Vltava and sailed under the Charles Bridge, your driving lessons for beginners were like spells of lyrical recreation compared with my impossibly congested Kartuska Street, or that training ground behind the vodka shop where we students were like actors rehearsing an avant-garde play before a tenacious audience.

"Not like that," said Miss Ciwle at last. "As soon as you stop chattering we crash into a post or the car stalls. Give it a touch more gas, please, let out the clutch slowly, and whatever you do don't change the angle of approach, the car'll take the bend itself. That's it, very good, slowly, easy does it." She placed her hands on mine and very gently pressed them to the steering wheel. "And please don't say another word now." "All right," I whispered, "but don't you reckon that if we must practise this blasted slalom we'd be better off driving forward than in reverse, because what sort of a snake crawls backwards? It's contrary to the laws of nature..."

My dear Mr Hrabal, I shall never forget what you wrote to me in your last letter but one, namely that the true connoisseur does not distinguish women according to the size of their breasts and buttocks, but by their hands, which was fully confirmed in this case, because Miss Ciwle, in her dark trousers and short leather jacket, did not look, as you once so delightfully put it, either like a bosomy or even less a bottomy babe – no, Miss Ciwle was rather slender in both respects and wasn't the sort of girl whose appearance prompts truck drivers to hit their nose against the steering wheel. That's just it – at first glance Miss Ciwle was the tomboy type, in whom luckily the spirit of progress had not yet wrought any permanent change, thanks to which she had beautiful chestnut hair tied in a ponytail, not a severe crew-cut; rather than a checked flannel shirt a silk blouse covered her girlish breasts, and on her feet, rather than heavy clod-hoppers, she had graceful pumps, almost as dainty and finely shaped as those long fingers of hers, which were pressing my hands to the steering wheel, thanks and thanks only to which I finally managed to drive in reverse to the end of that hellish slalom, until all the tosspots and winos standing behind the vodka shop gave me a cheer from the vicinity of some huge burdock leaves covering the shameless nudity of a stinking rubbish heap.

"So did they ever find the engine driver?" asked Miss Ciwle, taking a ready-made roll-up from her cigarette case. "Was he in hiding for long?" "He wasn't in hiding at all," I said, accepting the lighted cigarette from her with some surprise as she had only taken one drag on it herself. "He was just despairing in solitude, because he thought that was the end of his beautiful career, the end of his professional life, and that from the topmost rung of Jacob's ladder, from the atrium of railway heaven, as it were, he was going to fall to the very bottom of some repair shop. So he'd rented an upstairs room from Ajzensztok, the innkeeper at Żyrawka, and there in that room, which he didn't leave at all, he sat spinning a black web of thoughts about the fact that you never know where you are with Poles, because, as Fyodor Mikhailovich Dostoyevsky wrote a long time ago, the Poles are crafty and disloyal; at first they're all pally towards you, they pat you on the back and whisper sweet nothings in your ear, but next thing you know they're making fun of your Orthodox faith and imperfect accent. Such were engine driver Hnatiuk's bitter thoughts at Ajzensztok's inn, and he would have gone on brooding like that to the very end of his overdue leave, if not for Senior Constable Gwóźdź, who while drinking lemonade at the inn just happened to hear Hnatiuk's conversation with Ajzensztok through a half-open door, and in short," I said, handing Miss Ciwle the roll-up, "he detained the missing man and delivered him to the Railway Board, where he was handed the gold watch and one thousand five hundred zlotys reward out of the Chrzanów locomotive factory's special fund."

Yes, my dear Mr Hrabal, I had to break off my story for a while, because Miss Ciwle's tobacco was making my head spin, it was so strong and aromatic, but we soon got back into the Fiat and once I'd put it in first gear, as we were happily leaving the training ground, she asked: "So what about your grandmother's new Citroën?" "Oh, that was a real surprise," I said, managing by a miracle to turn left into Kartuska Street and shift into second gear without making a grating sound. "Hardly a day had gone by since the article in *The Times* when that evening the phone rang at my grandmother's flat. It was an inter-city call from Berlin, answered by her father – my great-grandfather Tadeusz – who was at once extremely perturbed, because down the line came the voice of his future son-in-law bellowing some dreadful things about Maria's funeral, to which his future father-in-law had not even condescended to summon his would-have-been son-in-law.

Not letting each other get a word in edgeways, they could neither ring off nor complete the conversation. The thing is, you see," I explained, "upon reading the report in *The Times*, which he bought at a tobacconist's on Potsdamer Platz, Karol had come to the direst conclusions, partly through the fault of the journalist, Mr Robinson, who in his colourful description of how the French tin-can was crushed by the Polish locomotive failed to say a single word about the miraculous salvation of the driving instructor and his student by Our Lady of Perpetual Succour – in other words, he thought he had lost his fiancée. Just imagine," I went on, jumping a red light, "they couldn't make each other understand, because every time my great-grandfather shouted into the phone in Lwów; 'But Maria's alive!', Karol yelled into the speaking-tube in Berlin that he had *The Times* broadsheet in front of him with the report and the photo, so would he please not try to deceive him – he was fully prepared for the worst." "Jesus," laughed Miss Ciwle, "couldn't he have asked your grandmother to come to the phone?" "Quite so," I said, timidly accelerating in second gear. "My grandmother was standing by the window and, on hearing the quarrel, made signs to her father to that effect, but not for long, because just as he was shouting 'But Maria's alive!', she noticed a brand new Citroën slowly coming up Ujejski Street and stopping outside their gate. Then she saw Mr Rosset, Citroën's representative, get out of it and check the house number against an address written on a little card. So when my great-grandfather finally decided to cut the knot of the conversation and shouted: 'All right, I'll call her to the phone right now!' she was no longer in the drawing room, but had gone into the study, the right place to receive the unexpected guest. So with some dismay her father said: 'She was here a moment ago, but now she's not,' to which his future son-in-law bawled back: 'Enough of these lies! Why won't you let me know the truth?', furiously slammed down the receiver, and was stared after all the way to the very door of the glazed speaking room by the amazed German operator.

"So that's how it looked," I went on, indicating right. "There stood my great-grandfather Tadeusz with the receiver in his hand, unable to believe the operator telling him the call was over, while my grandmother was standing in the study with Mr Rosset, unable to believe that the French firm was keen to give her a new car in exchange for an interview with *Le Monde*. Meanwhile Grandfather Karol was standing in the middle of Potsdamer Platz in Berlin holding a crumpled copy of *The Times*, unable to believe what his would-have-been, as he then supposed, father-in-law had said." "And now we're the ones standing," said Miss Ciwle calmly. "You didn't take the right-hand lane. I should have told you to, but can you be interrupted?" Indeed, more and more traffic was building up behind the Fiat, but there was a constant stream of cars coming down the right-hand lane, none of which would deign to let us through to turn off Kartuska Street into Sowiński Street, where the Corrado driving school was located, so despite the honking and the hostile gestures from the cars

behind, I was able to complete at least part of the story about
the new Citroën that Grandmother Maria really did get for
free. For what was the cost of the short interview she gave
next day to the reporter from *Le Monde*, in which she declared
that if she had stopped on the level crossing in any other car
she would never have lived to tell the tale, because neither a
Czech Tatra, nor a German Horch, nor a Polish Fiat, to say
nothing of an American Buick, had such smoothly opening
doors, making it easy to get out of the car safely a few seconds
before a collision, doors that save lives in any disaster. At this
point, at the reporter's suggestion, my grandmother told of
her nightmares about burning to death while trapped in a
Buick – if not for those doors, specially designed at the
Citroën factory by engineers who thought of everything, the
whole affair, so tendentiously described in *The Times*, would
have taken a truly tragic turn. So, standing by the new Citroën
in the glare of the magnesium flash, Grandmother Maria could
smile and optimistically avow that with Citroën she could
travel safely without worrying about bumps and potholes,
peasant carts, floods and hurricanes, or even locomotives.

I watched as Miss Ciwle battled with the door of her Fiat
and finally opened it; it was a fairly desperate act, because
although there was no express train tearing up on our right,
just cars, it did require some courage to stand in the right
lane, hold up the traffic like a policeman and beckon to me to
take advantage of the brief gap and turn quickly into Sowiński
Street, a manoeuvre that I performed almost to perfection,

almost, because once the little Fiat was gently rolling along the narrow street towards the Corrado school, the moment I caught sight in the mirror of Miss Ciwle smiling as she walked towards me, instead of stepping on the brake I trod on the accelerator. Before I had realised my mistake, the little car had lurched forward and mounted the right-hand kerb, and that was my first crash, my dear Mr Hrabal, a collision with a metal rubbish bin, which as well as a banana skin spilled out some cartons, rags, apple cores, cigarette butts, cans, bottles and newspapers and, who knows where from or why, an ebonite hand – a frightful body part from a tailor's dummy, whose detached wrist sported an enamel bracelet. "I can't leave you alone for a moment," cried Miss Ciwle, bending over the cracked right headlight. "It's impossible to teach you anything," she said, tapping the scratched paintwork. "Where are all your reporters from *The Times* and *Le Monde* now?" she continued, straightening the bent bumper with both hands. "Or maybe a Fiat dealer's going to pop up out of the blue and swap this scrap-heap of mine for a brand new one?" It was barely thirty metres to the Corrado school, so without looking round at me Miss Ciwle jumped into the car and moved up the narrow street, while I ran along the pavement after her injured little Fiat. I ran as fast as I could to try and reach the small parking area before she got out of the car – I wanted to open her door, bow down, fall to my knees and beg her forgiveness, promise to repair the damage and swear that never, ever again would I say another word about bygone eras and ancient cars.

But as soon as we stood facing each other by the open door of the Fiat, though I was out of breath from sprinting and she was upset about the breakage, I said: "Tomorrow I'll bring the cash for that light, but please don't be angry, please don't write me off, please don't send me packing, because no one teaches like you do." Then she smiled at me and replied: "No, they certainly don't. See you at the training ground at ten tomorrow morning. By the way, did Mr Czarzasty go on teaching your grandmother to drive?" "Oh yes," I answered eagerly, "except that he never again took the road over the level crossing."

My dear Mr Hrabal, you know better than anyone what true happiness is, that brief moment that we wouldn't swap for all the tea in China, that not-yet-realised but already-heralded moment when we can feel the benevolence of Fate, that same good-for-nothing Fate that doesn't favour us every day of the week. That's exactly how I felt right then as I walked down Sowiński Street – truly happy at the promise of my lessons to come with Miss Ciwle, and I felt just like your Gaston, who ran into the gypsy girl outside the window of the City Retail Trade on Main Street in Prague and knew it was no ordinary encounter, because it's not every day that you come across a gypsy girl outside the City Retail Trade on Main Street. So I picked up the dummy's hand with the enamel bracelet and walked to the bus stop on Kartuska Street, brimming with happiness and the scent of Miss Ciwle's hair, and all the sounds of the city, that whole terrifying rumble of

roaring trucks, trams and buses merging harmoniously into a
symphony full of the hopefulness of spring. If I had any regret,
it was only that I hadn't had time to tell Miss Ciwle the
conclusion of that story, because after the conversation with
his future father-in-law Grandfather Karol was convinced of
his fiancée's death and couldn't come to terms with the
thought that he'd been treated so appallingly – first that
they'd failed to inform him of the accident and the funeral,
and then that they'd lied to him on the telephone. He found it
inconceivable for such an upright person as Maria's father to
behave so improperly, and quite frankly, indecently. Why
hadn't he told him the truth, why had he lied?, Karol kept
thinking all night and all the next day, until at last, full of the
blackest thoughts, he bought a ticket and boarded the train.
When he changed trains in Warsaw to catch the express to
Lwów, he bought a few newspapers in the station hall,
including *Le Monde*, in which he saw a picture of his fiancée
standing beside a brand new Citroën. Immediately he ran to
the station post office to order a telegram to Berlin, in which
he asked his German friend Schwarz to send another one to
the Lwów address of his would-be father-in-law, saying: "Karol
deceased stop funeral day after tomorrow stop personal effects
deposited at Polish consulate for collection stop colleagues
from corporation in deepest sympathy stop". Having got this
message through to Schwarz, he managed to catch the express
to Lwów at the last second, and now felt completely calm
about the welcome awaiting him, because he really had

designed it all with an engineer's precision. Next morning as he was travelling by hackney cab from the main station with two bouquets of flowers he had bought, one a funeral wreath and the other a regular bunch, while as always on his return casting an affectionate eye about his home town, the flat on Ujejski Street was already in a state of pandemonium. Maria had fainted several times and the doctor had been summoned, Aunt Stasia was making cold compresses and looking for the smelling salts, and my great-grandfather Tadeusz had already placed an order for a telegram to the consulate in Berlin, and was nervously pacing the drawing room as he waited for a response, when the doorbell rang, and there stood Karol with his two bouquets. And then a real rumpus broke out, because when Maria shouted: "How could you do this to us?!" he produced first the page from *The Times* and then the page from *Le Monde* and asked: "And how could you do this to me?!" So they went on quarrelling loudly, and couldn't come to any sort of an understanding because every now and then one of them would cry out: "You don't love me!" to which the other would even more noisily object: "No, it's you that doesn't love me any more!" This fugue went on developing to and fro, until finally Maria handed Karol the keys of the new Citroën and said she never wanted to see him again because, just like a man, of course he was more interested in the fate of a car than his fiancée, at which he took offence, thrust both bouquets into the umbrella stand, said: "All right then, goodbye for ever!" then ran out of the building, jumped into the car and was off like a shot. And so, my dear Mr Hrabal, they would certainly have broken off their engagement for ever, which would have had fundamental significance for me, because I would have been someone completely different, and not their grandson many years later, but once again in Maria and Karol's life, and so in a way in my life too, the development of motor transport played a decisive role, because Grandfather Karol stepped hard on the gas just as the milkman's cart was emerging from the gates of the house next door. Grandfather slammed on the brakes, but those were Citroën brakes, block brakes rather than hydraulic, so the French marvel went smack bang into the pyramid of milk cans, there was a terrible grinding of flattened tin, a clatter of broken glass, and the horn was stuck blaring. Grandmother Maria, who had run out into the street after him to shout into the car's rear window: "And goodbye for ever to you too!", her hair streaming, was now rushing to the site of the accident, where she pulled her fiancé out of the sticky white ooze, stroked his bleeding forehead that had struck the windscreen and whispered: "Karol, my sweetheart, you're the only man I love in the whole world!" Trailing a broken right leg and leaning on her shoulder, he whispered that he'd never doubted it for an instant, and that more than anything in the world he loved her too. Then he added that never again would they sit together or separately in a Citroën or any other French car, because French technical thinking, just like French politics, is nonsense, nothing but empty swaggering, as evidenced by the

Maria and Karol's wedding in Lwów
"Karol, my sweetheart, you're the only man I love in the whole world!"

simple fact that despite having front-wheel drive, such a modern invention, the Citroën had archaic brakes that didn't stand up to the test in time of need, unlike the Horch, the Bentley or the Mercedes-Benz.

So my dear Mr Hrabal, next day the buses weren't running down to town from Ujeścisko because a water tank had been overturned near the pond and the police and the fire brigade had blocked off the road, so I was running across the fields to be on time for my second lesson with Miss Ciwle. High overhead I could hear the skylarks, and now and then partridges flew out of the grass underfoot, whirring away like saw blades. I had a book of your stories in my knapsack, one of which I wanted to recommend to my instructor, the one about evening driving lessons. I promised myself I wouldn't talk her into the ground this time, but I'd give her your book and say: "Here's a story teller before whom I bow down in silence." That was the plan I had ready, the discipline I meant to keep, but as soon as I came panting onto the training ground a minute after ten, Miss Ciwle smiled enigmatically, and before I'd started my parallel parking practice she'd handed me an identical copy of your stories and asked: "Do you read Hrabal? His stepfather Francin has something in common with your grandfather, if you're not making it up, of course."

I soon did all the exercises, and even the slalom went surprisingly well, but not once did she say "Well done", until finally she asked: "Are you cross with me for making that comparison?" We were standing smoking roll-ups in a patch of sunlight that divided the training ground in half. On the other side, three weary men were sitting over bottles of beer in the shade of a brick wall under a chestnut tree; they looked like nodding dervishes as they muttered their stories, with echoes of "fucking" and "bloody" rising into the sky like a steady stream of ardent prayer to the glory of the blazing morning sun.

"Grandfather Karol," I said at length, "never dismantled an engine himself and didn't trust motorbikes, nor did he ever make beer, just dynamite and other explosives – maybe that's why he didn't believe in progress and new inventions the way Francin did, though at times, just like Francin, he had some completely crazy ideas." "I knew it," said Miss Ciwle, all but giving me a kiss. "Get in again, please," she went on, putting out her roll-up on the asphalt, "turn right onto Kartuska Street, go a very short way and then turn left up the hill, keep going until you get to Warsaw Insurgents Street, then I'll tell you where to go next!" "I thought it'd just be the training ground today," I said, doing up my seatbelt. "I must confess, driving on the streets disgusts me." "Why on earth should it?" she chuckled as we set off. "Normally someone swears at you... once a week, I'd say," I explained, letting a tram pass in front of the little Fiat, "but once you take hold of this," I drummed my fingers on the steering wheel as I finally turned right into Kartuska Street, "in a single hour you hear as many 'fuck yous' as you normally get from your fellow man in the course of an entire year. I had no idea drivers were worse than monkeys, and I swear I was thinking of giving up – if it weren't for the Hrabal I brought across the fields for you today, there'd have been a fiasco, a desertion, I simply wouldn't have come any more. But as you hit upon the exact same idea, as you brought me the very same book, perhaps it means something, maybe it's a sort of sign, because as the Scriptures say, where two are gathered, at once there are three." "Watch out," she cut in sternly. "Please indicate left and wait until the cars opposite stop at the red light. Yes, that's good. So what about those crazy ideas of your grandfather's?" "The best one was with the wall," I replied at once, "that was one in a million, like the star turn from a comedy, and it all began with Mr Norbert who managed the Sanguszko estate and invited Grandfather to a wild pig hunt, at which the young chemical engineer got to know the young Prince Roman. As they stood in line waiting for the sow, they happened to start discussing what a terrible bore old aunts can be, because they both had the same problem of endless visits lasting several weeks at a time, visits paid by old aunts who not only disturbed their domestic harmony, but also adored motoring, and pestered their hosts with endless requests to be taken for a drive. So that's what they were chatting about as they stood waiting with their rifles loaded, until suddenly Grandfather Karol declared that if he had a palace like the Prince's, surrounded on all sides by a solid brick wall, he'd have solved the problem long ago. 'How do you mean?' said the Prince, adjusting his rifle. 'Very simple,' replied Grandfather, 'all I'd need would be a few workmen for a single afternoon and their total discretion.' " "Never — " said Miss Ciwle, winding down the window and lighting a roll-up. "Are you trying to tell me they walled her up in the family chapel like that wretched Mazepa chap? Surely times weren't like that any more, even if you were a prince?" "Of course it's got nothing to do with a chapel," I went on, "but a car drive, or in fact, the last drive ever taken by the Countess Euphemia, who was Prince Roman's unbearable aunt. So just listen to this: a few days before her arrival the master instructed Mr Norbert to fetch some craftsmen and smash a hole the width of the road in the south side of the park wall, then extend the road from the corner right up to the hole, eradicate all trace of the work and, in the empty gap where the mossy wall used to be, set up a cardboard decoy, which was all done most ingeniously. Finally the time came for the outing, and driving the Bugatti in his goggles and scarf, Prince Roman took that final bend, stepped on the gas and drove straight at the wall. 'Stop! Stop!' cried his aunt, 'where are you going?!' But the Prince just went on accelerating and called out: 'My goggles are covered in sweat, but this must be the gate, Auntie!' And they crashed into the wall, except that it was cardboard, and drove onto the park avenue with a huge piece of canvas on the bonnet, Prince Roman smiling and his aunt, the Countess Euphemia, half senseless with fear." "How awfully funny," snarled Miss Ciwle. "If I'd been the Prince's aunt I'd have whipped the rascal black and blue in front of everyone, like a snot-nosed brat. So did your grandfather's aunt get a hole in the wall too?" "How could she?" I said, shifting into first gear. "Grandfather Karol didn't have a palace and a park at his disposal, or that sort of wall, or a Bugatti sports car. He was still driving the *citron*, the one that spilled his blood and the Ukrainian milk on Ujejski Street, and his house was still under construction."

"Something doesn't quite fit here," said Miss Ciwle coolly. "If he didn't have a house, where did he receive that dreadful aunt of his? And where did he and your grandmother live? Surely they weren't still engaged all that time?" "It all fits," I said, when finally the third time the lights changed it was our turn and I was able to move sharply from the crossroads into Warsaw Insurgents Street. "He lived in a service house near the factory." "But wasn't the factory his?" Miss Ciwle wondered. "From your stories it sounds as if he was rich. How else does a man buy his fiancée a Citroën?" "That's dialectics and *Das Kapital* rolled into one," I replied, "because you should know that once my grandfather had returned to Lwów from Berlin after finishing his specialist studies, with a head full of ideas and the drafts for his future patents, his one small source of income had dried up – his single, tiny oil well on the edge of Borysław was refusing to cooperate, which was curious, because all the neighbouring wells were still oozing crude, while his had just stopped. So Grandfather poured all his savings into expert reports, the latest drill bits and having the well deepened, but all for nothing; the crude on his corner of Eldorado had come to a decisive end. That's how from being a modest owner of the means of production he became a unit of the manufacturing workforce, in other words a hired hand looking for employment, so straight after their wedding he and Maria moved to Chorzów, then to Warsaw, then back to Lwów; from there they went to the Free City of Danzig for a while, then to Warsaw again, then back to Lwów. By now Maria was on the verge of insanity, because the smaller their income, the bolder the plans my grandfather would dream up. 'Look,' he'd say, 'I've devised some new technologies – if we started using them in Poland, in twenty years we'd overtake the Germans.' But his wife's smile was a bitter one, because no one ever read those plans of his, while she, who adored flowers, was planting them in a different garden in a different city every year, so the whole thing didn't look too rosy."

I slowed down behind an old truck that was spewing out a monstrous cloud of exhaust fumes. "Only when Kwiatkowski began to build a factory at Mościce did Grandfather's designs prove useful, and that was where they finally settled down, first in a service villa near the factory, then in their own house." "Not bad," commented Miss Ciwle. "So what about his aunt? Unlike the countess, she must have gone on liking motoring?" "Oh yes," I said, moving down a gear smoothly this time, without the slightest grating sound. "Aunt Zofia came to stay with them at least three times a year from Borysław and always began by telling Grandfather to take her to Prince Sanguszko's palace at Gumniska – or rather not right up to the palace, but just as far as the park wall at the point where the solid bit had been set up again. She would get out of the car and walk down the dead-end turning to that spot, and put her hands against the wall, as if trying to convince herself it was no longer made of cardboard. Then she'd return to the Citroën, and as soon as Grandfather was speeding away, she would fulminate against such villainous behaviour, the times we live in, the decline of the aristocracy, the youth of today, the evils of Bolshevism, and the monstrosity of it all. Grandfather Karol would just keep accelerating, waiting for Aunt Zofia to make her ritual declaration: 'It's not the unfortunate woman who ended up in Bedlam that I pray for, but the young people who have no conscience, because as you can see, Karol, there are plenty of them about nowadays, even in our highest circles.' Grandfather would silently agree, and step even harder on the gas, because Aunt Zofia adored driving fast; deep down she regretted that Karol was not a prince and she a countess, and that they weren't tearing across Zbylitowska Hill in a Bugatti sports car the way Roman Sanguszko loved to."

The rickety truck, almost invisible behind its black cloud of exhaust fumes, which we had followed at a crawl up Warsaw Insurgents Street, suddenly snorted and, like an ancient mule that after years of labour refuses to obey a few moments before dying, came to a helpless standstill, blocking our lane. "Fantastic," said Miss Ciwle, discreetly glancing at her watch. "We won't move a kilometre before supper time!"

Indeed, my dear Mr Hrabal, we really were boxed in, and even if my instructor had jumped out of the Fiat like last time it wouldn't have done any good.

"So as for the *citron*," I calmly continued, "its days were already numbered, because to put his Aunt Zofia off these drives Grandfather Karol hit upon a brilliant idea, which was to take his Leica and a dozen rolls of film with him, and literally every few minutes he would stop the car, stand in the road, lie in the ditch, climb up a tree or vanish behind a hayrick and call out: 'Look, Aunt Zofia, what a wonderful frog!' or 'What a picturesque cow that is!' or 'That view of the clouds is worthy of Rembrandt!' while his aunt ran after him, also admiring everything, because what else could she do? So to discourage her even more, every time they got back to Mościce, Grandfather would suddenly look at his watch and cry: 'We'll just be in time to get them developed!' then turn the car around and rush across the bridge over the River Biała to Tarnów, to deliver the films to Chaskiel Bronstein for developing a couple of minutes before closing, because his studio on Krakowska Street was the best. Aunt Zofia, who didn't like Jews, had to look through the car windscreen at the shop front as Grandfather warmly greeted Mr Bronstein and collected the last set of pictures from him; then they would stand over just about every single photograph discussing the light exposure and the shutter speed, while she had to wait in the car, watching Grandfather get several new films and finally pay for it all, shake hands with Mr Bronstein and thank him not only for the service, but also for his professional advice. Altogether it often took more than half an hour, until finally Aunt Zofia rebelled against Grandfather's passion for photography, and when he dashed out of the car shouting: 'Just look at that girl in the headscarf – doesn't she look like a Hucuł highlander?' she stayed put with an offended look on her face. And that's what happened on the River Dunajec above Rożnów, where they went one afternoon. Grandfather leaped out of the car and started snapping away like a man possessed, because just then an RWD 6 aeroplane came flying over the valley and the skeleton of the newly erected dam, the sort of plane in which Żwirko and Wigura won the Challenge. Karol stood and watched this machine in total fascination, because suddenly that whole view of the hills, the river, the aeroplane and the dam had deeply touched his technician's soul – after all, that aeroplane, constructed in Mielec, was right up-to-date, the dam had been built at lightning speed and was also the latest design, and in his modest heart Grandfather felt something like an engineer's pride at the thought that in spite of all, this resurrected rubbish dump, this poor old country of his, even if rather slowly, was actually getting itself out of the doldrums, and maybe in twenty years' time it would be a significant place between Russia and Germany. That's how I imagine his euphoric state of mind," I said, looking Miss Ciwle in the eyes, "as he photographed that aeroplane gliding gently over the valley, with the dam and a forest of cranes in the background. Meanwhile the Citroën, though parked with the hand brake on, started to roll downhill. Aunt Zofia's cries and desperate waving were of no use as it picked up speed, raced towards the sloping riverbank and finally plunged into the Dunajec, none of which was noticed by the photography lover whose gaze was fixed on the sky. Only when the RWD 6 had disappeared over the horizon did Grandfather turn around and realise the gravity of the situation: the car was already steeped in water halfway up the doors, but it wasn't pond water, it was a rushing torrent, and the Citroën was drifting further from the bank by the second, while the terrified Aunt Zofia kept sounding the horn, then fruitlessly trying to push on the door. She was only saved by a miracle, because when the water had already reached the windows and Grandfather, up to his waist in it and having trouble keeping his balance, had proved just as unable to open the wretched door, the front wheel of the *citron* came to rest against an underwater boulder. Just then some workmen from the dam came running up and hauled on a rope tied to the back bumper; slowly, centimetre by centimetre, they tore the car from the grip of the current, and they would have completed the job if the rope hadn't snapped, but fortunately the car was already in far shallower water by then, allowing them to release Aunt Zofia from her trap and swiftly convey her on several manly shoulders to the stony shore, where the saved woman and her rescuers now stood and watched as the Citroën sank into the river for good and all."

"Didn't they try to get it out?" asked Miss Ciwle, lighting

another roll-up. "How deep is the Dunajec in its upper reaches?" "Not its upper, but its middle to lower reaches, besides which please consider the fact that at the time the dam was almost finished and they had just started testing it by stemming the flow of the water at Rożnów, on top of which Grandfather Karol refused even to think of it. As soon as his aunt had left for Borysław he immediately got in touch with Citroën's representative for southern Poland and told him about the defective braking system, with particular regard to the hand brake in automobiles produced by his firm, but Mr Rosset politely replied that this incident was not the result of manufacturing faults, but poor utilisation. Evidently, the good fortune Maria had enjoyed in Lwów was not to befall Karol in Mościce, because by now Citroën was selling far more cars in Poland and had a new advertising campaign, quite apart from which," I said, handing Miss Ciwle the ashtray, "can salvation on a level crossing really be compared with a stony beach on the River Dunajec, can a picture of a young lady *automobiliste, la belle polonaise*, be compared with one of a corpulent middle-aged engineer? So to conclude the conversation my grandfather stated dryly that from now on he would choose an Austrian Steyr, a Czech Tatra, a Polish or Italian Fiat over any French car, because the Steyr, the Tatra and even the Polish Fiat had hydraulic brakes, while Citroën still insisted on those archaic cables, which meant that each wheel braked separately, and the discs were never all locked with equal force." "So what did he drive after that?" asked Miss Ciwle, passing back the ashtray. "What make?" "It was a Mercedes-Benz 170 V," I replied, "with a beautiful moss-green body." "So it wasn't a Polish Fiat?" Miss Ciwle was laughing out loud now. "Too small, or too expensive?" "Too expensive for such a small car," I replied without a second thought, "just like your little beauty here." "What'll you have after your test?" "Oh, I'll keep taking the bus, in time I'll earn enough for a bike, and after that it's got to be a hang-glider." "So why do you want a driving licence?" "Good point," I said, nodding at the mirror, which reflected a kilometre-long queue snaking behind us. "Probably merely to be able to ponder, for example, the meaning of Confucius's strange saying that if courtesy and music aren't flourishing, forfeits and penalties are unjust." "How you do go on!" she said, laughing. "Isn't there a simpler way of talking about traffic fines?"

My dear Mr Hrabal, you can't begin to imagine what a rush of emotion came over me next moment – I very nearly let the Fiat off the clutch, we very nearly smashed into the back of that blasted truck, which despite being stationary was still blowing a dreadful cloud of dense fumes straight up our noses – all because, having asked that rhetorical question, Miss Ciwle glanced at her watch and immediately added: "Right, let's get over to my place." At once she began to move into the driver's seat over my knees, while just like the first time, I had to shift across into the passenger seat beneath her. Once this reshuffle had taken place, Miss Ciwle reversed the Fiat about a dozen centimetres, virtually under the bumper of the Trabant

behind us, shifted into first gear, turned the steering wheel as
far right as it would go and slowly, ever so slowly extracted us
from our snare, drove the Fiat onto the pavement, tactfully let
some pedestrians go by, then drove onto the lawn, where she
accelerated sharply; once she'd got us past the truck she
slowed down and crossed the pavement again, nipping back
onto the road. Not only was it a masterful manoeuvre, but as I
realised a moment later when I glanced in the mirror, it was a
true deliverance, because it turned out the truck not only had
a broken engine and gearbox, but also faulty brakes; seconds
after we had bailed out of the traffic jam it had started rolling
sluggishly downhill, crumpling the nose of the Trabant; the
Trabant had flattened the front of the Beetle, the Beetle had
dented the Toyota, the Toyota the Opel, and thus, like billiard
balls or dominoes given a shove by an invisible finger the cars
were knocking into each other; this steady linear motion
seemed to have no end, just as Isaac Newton described it long
ago.

Meanwhile Miss Ciwle had stepped on the gas and at the
very first crossroads turned right, so now we were driving fast
alongside the Napoleonic forts. I could see she was getting
more and more fretful, now and then glancing at her watch
and the speedometer, as if we were covering a stretch of the
Paris–Dakar rally. After a while we turned into the allotments
on the hills and she drove even faster; her little Fiat bounced
over the holes in the road like a ball, and I wondered what the
hurry was for, because it could have meant all sorts of

different things. But none of my assumptions proved correct, my dear Mr Hrabal, for when we literally fell into a small allotment surrounding a wooden shed with an adjoining lean-to, Miss Ciwle said: "Please wait here – I have to give my brother an injection." And when a few minutes later I saw her emerge from the shed, pushing a wheelchair with a smiling young fellow in it, when she introduced us to each other I suddenly realised that the wooden shed with the lean-to was their permanent home and that they had no other. "Would you like a coffee?" she said. "Not inside, you'd be shocked by the mess, but Jarek" – she pointed to her brother – "is dying to hear your stories about old cars; when I told him about the *citron* and the level crossing he almost stood up from his chair. He understands everything, but if he tries to say something it just comes out as 'uuu' or 'aaa'. I'll be back in a moment – but maybe you're in a hurry? I can take you to the bus stop first, if you prefer. Everything's running late today because of that bloody truck." Soon after she emerged from the shed carrying a tray with a pot of coffee, two mugs, some biscuits and a plate of porridge. "So what about the Mercedes?" she asked. "Did it have better brakes than the *citron*?"

My dear Mr Hrabal, why deny it? I was completely thrown by this unusual situation: Miss Ciwle was feeding Jarek with a tablespoon which she put down every now and then to take a sip of coffee from her mug, while I gazed all around me, staring past the trees in the allotments and the wildly overgrown cemetery at the incredibly beautiful

pattern formed on the spring air by the brick towers of the
Hanseatic churches that stood out on the city skyline. "It
had good brakes," I finally replied, "but just imagine how
complicated servicing a car was in those days." "Nonsense,
it can't possibly have been that bad," she said huffily. "They
must have done away with the gear pedals and the ignition
lever by then and just like today you had brakes, a clutch and
an accelerator." "That's right," I replied, dunking a bit of
biscuit in my coffee, "but nowadays you only have to do the
first inspection after fifteen thousand kilometres – in those
days the driver literally never parted company with the
instruction manual; he probably wrote it all down in his
diary at once. For example" – I listed from the beginning –
"for that 170 model every five hundred kilometres you had
to check the fan-belt tension, then the oil and the coolant,
and finally the braking for all four wheels. Every one
thousand five hundred kilometres you had to change the
engine oil, clean out the air filter net, lubricate the clutch,
brake, accelerator and starter levers and top up the oil in the
central lubrication tank. Every four-and-a-half thousand
kilometres you had to remove and clean out the fuel filter,
check the carburettor and throttle, and the slack in the
engine bolts. Every seven-and-a-half thousand you had to
change the oil in the gearbox, change the oil filter and fill
the rear wheel bearing covers with lubricating oil; and every
fifteen thousand kilometres you had to rinse out the cooling
system, lubricate the front springs and position the brake

shoes with the correct amount of slack, not to mention that after one hundred thousand the cylinders were ready for grinding and polishing." "Stop!" said Miss Ciwle, putting the spoon and plate on the table, while Jarek mumbled something. "He wants to hear more," she went on, turning to face me, "but we don't want to bother you. He's had his injection and his food now, so let's drive down the hill to the bus stop." "No, please stay here," I said. "It's not far, I'll go on my own." "You've paid for an hour's driving," she protested, "so we must finish the lesson. I'll just set up my brother's reading, then we can go." "We could always make the next lesson twenty minutes longer," I said, not eager to take the steering wheel again. "I'll be off for today." "Fine, I'll walk down a short way with you, as far as the shop," she said, giving in. "I'll just get his book ready."

A few minutes later we were marching down the lane between the allotments, as the Hanseatic church towers grew smaller and smaller before vanishing from sight, but I hardly noticed them as I walked down the cemetery fence, past the rows of sheds and cabins which, as the TV aerials, tin chimneys, hencoops and outhouses showed, were not summer cottages at all, but permanent homes. Instead of church towers I was thinking about the people who must have had frozen taps, smoking stoves, leaking roofs and blown fuses here in winter, the people who lived here among the trees and bushes, as if on the roof of our city, though they were far from being Olympians. "Why are you so quiet?" asked Miss Ciwle.

"Nothing to say when you're a foot soldier?" "Not at all," I shrugged, "I'm just in the mood for listening instead of talking." "You're shocked," she said in a matter-of-fact way. "They don't show estates like ours on TV, and what'd we have to advertise anyway? The air perhaps, but they're not selling it – yet," she smiled to herself, "and when they start to, they'll build houses here for people with some cash."

And that, my dear Mr Hrabal, was the end of our walk and our conversation; Miss Ciwle went into the shop, and I went on marching down to Warsaw Insurgents Street, where the firemen were busy cutting the interlocked cars apart, causing an even bigger traffic jam than before. I tell you, it was beautiful, with great plumes of sparks flying from under the whirling blades like the tresses of Berenice's hair, so very beautiful that I slowed down and, despite my own principles, joined the dense crowd of gawpers who actually gasped in delight every time an ambulance drove up to fetch the latest driver to be extracted from that metal tangle. I couldn't get my head straight, I couldn't relax – not because of the poor devils being laid out on stretchers and carted off to hospital, but the scene I had witnessed through the door of Miss Ciwle's wooden shed: she'd positioned her brother's wheelchair near the window, and on a stand like the ones musicians use for their music, she'd put a book at exactly the height of his eyes, then hung a sort of dog-collar round his neck, with a flipper hanging on a spring, and it was incredible to see how that crippled brother of hers tossed his head a bit, grabbed the metal flipper in his mouth, then freely turned the pages of the book with it, looking for the point where he'd stopped reading last time. It was extraordinary to watch him stop and wonder "Have I read this bit before?", then shuffle the pages of your stories with that pointer, my dear Mr Hrabal, until finally he found the right place, let go of the pointer and began reading, smiling from ear to ear. Meanwhile Miss Ciwle was getting ready to go out, touching up her discreet make-up before a small mirror hanging on the wall, because – as I have already told you – she had to go down the hill with me, as far as the little shop at the foot of the allotments. Yes, I was amazed to glimpse an intimate moment in their life, no doubt a quite ordinary one for them, and when Miss Ciwle had done her make-up, I was amazed to step back from the window and accidentally tread on a small green bushy plant, a sprawling weed hidden amid the convolvulus and gooseberries. I stepped aside in confusion, only to notice some similar weeds cunningly planted in the sunniest spots, but even better concealed from the stares of the neighbours among the blackcurrant bushes, rampant wild flowers and clumps of gladioli and peonies. Yes, I was amazed to see such a plantation of the sacred herb that made its way to us from India, and is still persecuted just as Dionysus once was in Greece.

The firemen had just finished cutting up the last car, this time freeing an uninjured driver, as the disappointed crowd of gawpers passively looked on. I went on my way to the bus stop, to go home to Ujeścisko, planning as soon as I got there

to unearth those two or three photographs from the past, all
that I had left from my grandparents, and at my next lesson to
show Miss Ciwle Grandmother Maria's *citron* and Grandfather
Karol's Mercedes, or rather not so much her, as Jarek, who
might find those photographs really interesting, and might get
pleasure from them too. But I searched in vain; the pictures
were nowhere to be found. I guessed they'd probably got lost
during the move when Anula and I left Chrzanowski Street for
Ujeścisko; they'd probably made their way into the dustbin
with a pile of old newspapers, letters and bills, so I'd probably
only be able to tell Miss Ciwle about them during our next
drive, and I was sorry somehow, I felt truly disinherited, for
what are losing your house or your property compared with
losing your only souvenir photographs? I went to my next
lesson feeling mightily depressed, resolved not to say another
word to my instructor about motoring tales of yore, not a
whisper – ever since I'd lost those photos I felt as if I'd been
robbed of literally everything.

But my dear Mr Hrabal, fate was to deal me yet another
surprise, because I got off the bus on the corner of Kartuska
Street and walked up Sowiński Street, mentally composing the
first sentence I would say to Miss Ciwle that day: "Please
forgive me, but the loss of some family photographs has put
me in a state of deep melancholy, so please don't ask me any
questions, don't say a word, not a syllable, not a squeak...!" –
but when thus prepared I reached the Corrado driving school,
Instructor Uglymug leaned his prematurely grey head out of

his small Fiat and said: "You're the writer, aren't you? Over here, please, Miss Ciwle had to take the day off. So let's see what the results of the female teaching are."

My dear Mr Hrabal, I instantly felt the same as during my first lesson, as if life had turned another circle and suddenly I was back at a familiar point. "Just with the way you get into the car you can make a prat of yourself," boomed Instructor Uglymug when I got myself tangled in too loose, too long a seatbelt. "You might only need one hand to play pocket billiards," he said, helping me do up the buckle. "But you're not at the polytechnic now – with driving you've got to think," he virtually bawled at me when the engine stalled at my first attempt to start it. "A driver's got to have balls," he chortled, very pleased with himself, "not a pair of frilly knickers! Hasn't our Iron Lady deflowered you yet, our proper little pricktease, our saintly sex kitten at the wheel?" "No," I snarled angrily. "You shut up, Uglymug, because I'm not remotely interested in your aesthetic views, and if you get on my nerves I'll bugger up your car at the first crossroads." My dear Mr Hrabal, I was amazed at myself, wondering where on earth I'd got such language and confidence from, where on earth such winged and boundless boorishness had suddenly come from. But of course it was an error that cost me dearly, because as soon as he heard me talk like that, Uglymug, the wretched scum, immediately took me for one of his own, and I sure got what I deserved. Yes, Mr Hrabal, it took me straight back to the army, it was pure *déjà vu*, a sentimental journey to the heart of my time at university, because while driving the little Fiat with Instructor Uglymug, who kept clapping me on the shoulder and bawling filthy jokes in my ear, I was reminded of misty mornings when I marched through sleepy Wrzeszcz, down Lelewel Street to the Military Department, stood to attention in a line, then marched into the lecture hall, where Major Bushy-Tache educated us about the disastrous effects of long hair on national security, Lieutenant Gewgaw responded to a nuclear attack, and Colonel Pitchfork cast light on the imponderabilia of Lenin's and Brezhnev's doctrines. They all spoke more or less like Instructor Uglymug, they all had the same way of guffawing at their own jokes, the same way of winking at us knowingly as soon as one of two immortal topics – namely boozing or fucking – came up in their digressions, and the same way of wanting to be pally with us, while in actual fact they despised everything that to their minds bore the faintest whiff of the humanities faculty.

"I used to work here," said Uglymug, interrupting my military reverie and pointing to a neon sign, switched off at this time of day, announcing the Lida bar. "There used to be some cash to be made around here. Whenever one of those suckers pulled a bird, and wanted a quick ride to a cheap motel, I did the driving, but now that bastard's built an upstairs, now he's got those rooms by the hour, they don't need transport any more, and you know what, I had to sell the cab, so now I slog away at this shit with the likes of you. But they say you're a writer," Uglymug burst into noisy laughter, "you must come here often – what better story can you get than some slut going on about her miserable life? Oh, I've got a tale or two to tell all right – if you happen to know any film directors I could give them a box office hit. Take this bird Viola, she used to be your common slapper at the port, then she brushed up her act at the Monopol, and when she turned up on the dance floor at the Lida, it was Hollywood on Kartuska Street. But you know what, she fell madly in love with a poof, so much she had an operation done and became a bloke, so nowadays she sucks him off as Valentine not Viola, because that's the name she had written in her ID, and that nancy boy of hers is a waiter – when they threw him out of the Lida he moved to the Cristal. Can you imagine changing sex for love? Well, fuck me, that's the sort of thing you should write about, not about the commie era like they all do nowadays. The commie era wasn't bad at all, people've just got spoiled now, and I'll tell you a fact, it's the worst thing when you don't keep 'em in tight check, because it's a right brothel now, none of your freedom. Take cars, say: they've bought so many of them now there's no getting anywhere, it's just one big traffic jam from dawn to dusk, but if you brought back rationing there'd only be as many motors as there's room for on the roads."

My dear Mr Hrabal, I was silent as we stood at the lights by the Lida bar, and at the training ground, and finally on the way back down Kartuska Street, from where I turned perfectly smoothly into Sowiński Street and drove up to the Corrado

school. I was silent the next day too, when Miss Ciwle wasn't
at work again and I had to take the wheel of Instructor
Uglymug's car again, and I was silent after the lesson too, as I
climbed the hill spread above the city like Elijah's cloak in the
Bible, lined with a pattern of little cabins and a chessboard of
allotments, where the lilac and thyme were already in bloom,
where old bathtubs covered in moss were waiting for some
rainwater, where children were shouting and the odours of
dinner were floating on the air, along with the clatter of pots
and the lazy, afternoon cackle of hens. I was still silent as I
walked up to the window of Miss Ciwle and her brother
Jarek's wooden shed, where no one was at home, so in just as
much silence I wrote a little card and shoved it in the door:
"Please call me, I'm in the clutches of Instructor Uglymug."
And in even greater silence I walked downhill along the old
cemetery towards the city, above which a cloud of exhaust
fumes was now obscuring the sun and the brick-red Gothic of
the Hanseatic churches. Yes, Mr Hrabal, I really was Instructor
Uglymug's hostage and I was sorry I had ever enrolled in the
course, because although it was possible to change teachers at
your own request, it always meant failing the final test at least
three times, and as a result inevitably having to repeat the
course. So I gritted my teeth and, just like at military studies, I
pretended to be extremely interested, like a snake deluding a
despot; every time Instructor Uglymug told a joke I burst out
laughing, every time he trotted out an anecdote I switched off
my hearing and concentrated on driving the car, which I was

doing better and better at any rate. I shall merely add that what's known as the post-training Dovzhenko-Down effect was the same as after eight hours of drill in our university army, namely, the need to wet your whistle.

Oh, my dear Mr Hrabal, if only we'd had the chance to visit those beloved beer halls of yours in those days, if only instead of the piss served in Gdańsk we'd been able to drink a refrigerated Branik or a Velkopopovicky Kozel or a Staropramen, or just an ordinary Pilsner, maybe we'd have grown up into completely different people, but yes, every Thursday after military studies, when we simply had to purge ourselves of those eight hours of idiocy, we set off on a tour, starting at Jurek's on the corner of Danusia Street, then moved to The Cobblers on Lendzion Street; next we wended our way to Agata's on Grunwaldzka Avenue, and finally got wrecked at The Catholic on Hübner. If anyone had failed to get plastered, there was still the Lońka by the railway tracks, or the Lilliput opposite the Eternal Flame Cinema as the innermost circle of hell, and all those low dives, all those rutting grounds, all those sewers founded in Bierut's time, flourishing in Gomułka's and breathing their last in the mature Gierek era, all those stations of the cross of ours came back to me now, as I sat at the wheel of Instructor Uglymug's little Fiat. Minute by minute I grew more and more thirsty for the smell and taste of beer, which even if it was rubbish, and watered down to boot, still bore an undeniably Dionysian lustre – the lustre of youth, gifted us only once in a lifetime.

That's just how it was, my dear Mr Hrabal, as soon as the hour's driving was over and I was free of the grip of Instructor Uglymug, I had to have a drink immediately, so I asked him to drop me off somewhere in the city centre, because on Kartuska Street there were a few all-night shops open, but not a single bar. So I went straight to the Istra, then the Starówka bar near the bike shop, then to the Cotton, which only opened at four pm, and every time I demanded a different kind of beer and checked, quite like your stepfather Francin, if the glass was perfectly clean, if the beer was at the right temperature, and if the foam was thick enough.

After several such tests I was completely disgusted and sank into deep melancholy, because everything was in the best possible order, in ideal harmony, sterile and ship-shape, and although I should have been glad of it, because ultimately can there be any greater pleasure than, for instance, trying the first sip of Heweliusz on the tip of your tongue, then Żywiec, then Guinness, can there be any greater pleasure than comparing how much and what sort of malt was used in each of those brands, what sort of soil the barley grew in, and how many days' sun last year's hops enjoyed? There really can't, and if in spite of that I sank into deep melancholy, the reason was obvious: once again I had realised, my dear Mr Hrabal, that everything in my life had come too late, after the event, and thus as it were needlessly and senselessly; but then I remembered your job at the steelworks, or the time when you were a "writer in liquidation", or the wedding at Libni, and somehow my mood passed, somehow I flushed out my melancholy and Instructor Uglymug's smell of infected gums and sweaty polo shirts and, as I sat outside at the Istra bar, from where I could admire the gates of the Arsenal and the crowds of German pensioners, or as I watched the billiard table at the Cotton, I remembered how at Jurek's on Danusia Street Atanazy the poet used to borrow an accordion from the local dwarf and play Ukrainian *dumki* and Bielorussian *chastushki*, and at once, almost instantly, the air, grey with coarse tobacco smoke, would turn bright blue. Outside in the street people would stop and stare in delight through the arched, Moorish little windows into the pitch-dark interior of the bar, while Atanazy, for whom the regulars would pour vodka into a beer mug for his playing, would get into the swing of it and go on in Gypsy style: *Oy, they love, they love horses* or *When trouble comes round again*, and in this way he'd crank up the atmosphere, until it was all set for a few of our favourite patriotic songs, which were soon being sung at full volume by the languorous crowd of drunkards. For those few minutes they all became one big family, fell into each other's arms and patted each other on the back shouting: "Next year in a free Poland!" as they wiped away their tears, until finally the terrified Jurek made hand signals to say that was enough. So we'd go outside, carrying Atanazy in our arms while at the top of his voice he recited poetry by Adam Mickiewicz so beautifully and so loud that windows and Secession-style balcony doors would open, and we'd be showered in flowers.

Then Atanazy would start reciting *Papa's Return* da capo, and more or less the twenty-second time that famous father returned, we'd reach The Cobblers on Lendzion Street, where the exhausted Atanazy usually fell asleep after the very first shot of vodka.

Meanwhile we'd cajole ex-General Starveling, who had nowhere to live and sat it out at The Cobblers from opening to closing, into telling us about the raid on the GDR again, and we'd revel in the story of how instead of landing at Wolin as part of the "Shield" manoeuvres, our Gdańsk marine corps shifted a little further west, and at five hours forty-three commenced artillery fire and landings on the East German coast, which caused panic not only among the combine drivers from the Liebknecht Agricultural Cooperative, who just at that moment were driving along the Baltic shore to the nearby rape fields, but also at Warsaw Pact headquarters in Berlin, Moscow and Warsaw. "What the hell do you think you're doing, you stupid Polaks?!" yelled Nikita Sergeyevich Khrushchev down the phone. "But Comrade," said Wiesław Gomułka, wrested from sleep and having trouble finding his glasses, without which he couldn't utter a word, "Comrade Nikita Sergeyevich, you wanted sweetcorn, so all our state farms are sowing nothing but sweetcorn now, and lots of individual farmers are starting to sow it too." "I'll give you individual sweetcorn, damn you!" interrupted the infuriated Nikita Sergeyevich. "I'll remind you of the Ribbentrop-Molotov pact! You must be out of your minds to go attacking the GDR, and at five forty-five in the morning too!" And then ex-General Starveling told us with great dignity how he was demoted, and how the prosecutor demanded the death penalty, not for the unfortunate, alcohol-induced raid on GDR terrain, but for being insolent before the court martial, where General Starveling had stated as fact that it hadn't been a mistake at all, but his, a Polish general's personal response to the volleys fired by the battleship *Schleswig-Holstein*, which by bombarding Westerplatte had not only started the Second World War but also cut short his childhood and deprived him of seventeen relatives, all shot at Piaśnica, Stutthof and Auschwitz.

So as soon as the ex-General's story had reached its end once more, we fetched Atanazy the poet from his chair by the wall and carried him, rolled up like a carpet, to Agata's bar, where he gradually came to, listening to Mr Żakiewicz telling us about his dear old auntie who was driven out of Wilno by the Bolsheviks and had settled in Kashubia, a woman so enchanting, so full of magical charm that even her farmyard pigs, ducks, hens and dogs stopped understanding Kashubian and converted to her sing-song borderlands Polish, full of warmth, radiance and archaic nobility – in short, a woman so refined and bewitching that Ryszard Stryjec, who was sitting at Mr Żakiewicz's table, immediately took a napkin and in a few bold strokes drew the lady's portrait. It was amazing to watch the artist sketching nothing less than a holy Byzantine icon – he drew an ordinary woman in a Kashubian farmyard, and at the same time a Madonna in the style of Caravaggio. Whenever I think of that scene at Agata's bar, where our poet Atanazy gradually came to under the influence of the conversation between those two castaways from Atlantis, it occurs to me, my dear Mr Hrabal, that never and nowhere could I ever have seen anything as entrancing as those few simple lines drawn on that little napkin, creating a synthesis of East and West out of something real and natural, as well as beautiful.

But it was already time to be moving on, to The Catholic, where all the other castaways from the military used to gather: Pitek the poet whose verses were always about his latest girlfriend's menstrual blood, the introverted poet Salim, who only wrote in Sanskrit, von Bock, who wrote mathematical poems, and also the long-distance epic bore, one Dimski-Witski, who could trace his genealogy back to the Kashubian aristocracy, which didn't impress us in the least, because we knew perfectly well, my dear Mr Hrabal, that just as the entire Czech aristocracy was wiped out at the Battle of White Mountain, so too the Kashubian aristocracy all bled to death at the Siege of Vienna, nevertheless beating the Turks under the extremely lucky star of King Jan Sobieski. So we chattered freely among ourselves about that and other things, and wondered why Günter Grass, who as a fourteen-year-old used to run about the same streets as us in Wrzeszcz, never wrote a great historical novel about the heroic Kashubians – as most of them fell at the Siege of Vienna, what, or rather who else should the debutant Günter Grass, of 13 Labesweg, nowadays

Lelewel Street, have written about? How might he have evoked the warring spirit of the Samurais through a race reduced to the peasantry in such a tragic way? But those conversations of ours at The Catholic always came to a hasty end, because once rested and invigorated, Atanazy the poet would ostentatiously start blowing on the palm of his hand, turn up his cuff and, showing off his sinewy forearm, challenge an opponent. Once it was a manager from the Katowice steelworks, once it was an animal tamer from the Arena Circus, another time it was a sailor from a Finnish freighter. We always took bets, and never lost, because Atanazy looked like a weakling, so anyone who had never dropped into The Catholic before usually bet ten to one against him, whereas those who knew his method hoped to witness his very first defeat. But Atanazy was infallible and never lost, and that was because in the culminating stage, when the interlocked hands were jammed at a standstill over the table top like a hammer and sickle, and everything was still in the balance, in his booming, metallic voice Atanazy would start reciting: "Phlebas the Phoenician, a fortnight dead..." He'd break off for a moment, then go on, staring hard at his opponent – "Forgot the cry of gulls, and the deep sea swell, and the profit and loss. A current under sea picked his bones in whispers..." and that was the moment when he gained the advantage – not always overwhelming, but the clear advantage – because even though none of Atanazy's opponents knew Eliot's poem, they were shocked by the image of the carcass of some Phoenician with his eyes eaten up by salt and eels, carried away by the currents like a swollen, stinking balloon, and when Atanazy roared at full voice: "Gentile or Jew, O you who turn the wheel and look to windward, consider Phlebas, who was once handsome and tall as you" – his opponent's hand went limp; seconds later it fell to the table top, and we could gather up the bets.

But who could I tell about it now, my dear Mr Hrabal? Ewa at the Istra? The barman at the Cotton? The German pensioners on an outing, wending their way from the Arsenal along the River Motława? How could they possibly be interested in our military Thursdays, our suburban bacchanals, our thrills and spills that there's nothing left of any more? So I sank deeper and deeper into complete melancholy, and after each lesson with Instructor Uglymug, who kept doubling and trebling his efforts to enrol me in his new political party, the thirtieth in a row, after every hour of this kind I went to purge my soul at a bar. I had a heavy heart, not just because of the weight of my memories, but also because I was pining: at the Corrado office they told me Miss Ciwle had taken unpaid leave, they didn't know how long for. Apparently she'd gone to get her brother treated, but they didn't know where, or else they didn't want to tell me, so once again I went to the hills where her shed stood in silence like a barque submerged in time and foliage; grass had already started growing in the ruts carved out by the tyres of the Fiat, new spider webs had been spun in the window of the lean-to, the rainwater in the washtub was coated in duckweed, hedgehogs were running riot under the currant bushes, and all around May was bursting forth with the scent of lilac, the song of thrushes and the trill of an oriole. Even the city with its stench of exhaust fumes could not restrain this burgeoning, which I could also see in the frenzied, as if febrile growth of the Indian herb: its exuberant sprays and succulent stems seemed to be swelling by the minute, as if ripening in an unnatural, frantic rush, faster than the mystery contained in them since the beginning of time. So, my dear Mr Hrabal, I picked a few of those sacred stems, the ripest ones, to give back to Miss Ciwle when she got home – she was sure to be extremely disappointed by such premature sprouting and the waste of her crop.

Holding my weeds, I set off along the fence surrounding the cemetery, where the poor devils killed in the First World War lay at rest, which must have been why I thought of Grandfather Karol again, not as a motorist this time but as a gunner in the invincible Royal Imperial Austro-Hungarian Army. After a mustard gas attack he made it to the field hospital, where he lay unconscious for more than twelve hours; when he awoke, he looked up and saw a nun's wimple, whiter than Alpine snow, and cried out: "Water, please, Sister, water!" Then the nun handed him a glass and said: "First you should make your confession." Grandfather Karol clutched at his head and realised he looked like a mummy – not a single hair was left of his luxuriant mane, because along with his gas

...I thought of Grandfather Karol again, not as a motorist this time but as a gunner in the invincible Royal Imperial Austro-Hungarian Army. (Grandfather Karol is first on the right)

mask the orderly who rescued him had removed all his hair, which had fallen out as an effect of the gas. But though wounded and bald, Grandfather Karol desperately wanted to live and told the nun: "I've no intention of dying, so I won't be making my confession." At that she took offence, and when all the seriously wounded patients were given morphine she manipulated matters to leave him out, so he suffered appalling, unmitigated pain, but he didn't give in or make his confession. Finally he recovered enough to go home to Lwów for further treatment, and even his hair grew back, except that it was flame red now. That's what I was thinking about on Warsaw Insurgents Street, as I shook my spray of greenery at a car that almost ran me over – I thought that if at the time he'd had some dried leaves from Miss Ciwle's allotment in his cigarette case he'd have had a much easier time in that field hospital; in his nocturnal ramblings he wouldn't have had nightmares about the trenches, but much pleasanter dreams, about picnics in Żyrawiec or skiing in Truskawiec, trips the Polytechnic students and professors used to go on, so if he saw me now he certainly wouldn't think badly of me for getting on the bus with my bunch of Indian herbs, punching my ticket and sitting in an empty seat behind the driver, among the widows with their pots and flowers who'd been on their daily visit to their husbands at the cemetery. Oh yes, I could imagine him smiling when one of the old ladies asked me if the plant I was holding was good for a hedgerow, or maybe for growing seedlings in a frame, because although

Grandfather Karol was never an anarchist, he didn't like officials and their bans, he didn't like stupid politicians and he would certainly have been most surprised that in our country the Pharisees in charge permit and encourage us to worship Dionysus at any time of day and anywhere we like, including Parliament, and yet they persecute Shiva. Yes, my dear Mr Hrabal, it's just as if we're not free to choose our own gods, as if we all have to revere the same, single despot that's imposed on us in the form of excise duty and VAT. Then suddenly, on the road to Ujeścisko, I had an inspiration and the scales fell from my eyes like Saul as I caught sight of a new land and a new sky, and myself swathed in a grey cloud, because I had just remembered de Quincey and his visions, so as soon as I got home I put the green weeds in the sunniest spot on the balcony to dry out nicely, then they could be cut up and crumbled, and finally smoked. Just as I was closing the balcony door, wondering how long it would take, the phone rang and I heard Miss Ciwle at the other end, asking me in that slightly metallic voice of hers if I was still in the clutches of Inspector Uglymug and if I'd like to get free of them, because she was back now and at my disposal. That's just what she said, my dear Mr Hrabal: "I'm at your disposal." I was a whisker away from shouting down the phone about the weeds I'd picked outside her shed, which were now drying on my balcony, but I bit my tongue and said: "I want to have a lesson with you right now, do you hear me, right now!" at which she burst into mocking laughter and answered: "All right, but it'll be an evening driving lesson, what do you say to that?"

Soon we'd agreed to meet at a quarter to eight by the all-night shop at the training ground, where I was ready and waiting right on the dot, watching the winos leaping about in ecstasy against the setting sun. This time they didn't look like dervishes, but members of Saint Vitus's sect; at the sight of the little Fiat and my instructress getting out of it they reached the absolute zenith of their mystical potential, shouting unintelligible incantations, waving their arms about and falling to the floor. "What a madhouse," said the disgusted Miss Ciwle. "Never mind, let's make tracks." So we did, my dear Mr Hrabal, at high speed, because at that time of day there was no traffic on Kartuska Street, and I guess I was driving pretty well by then. "Well, well, well," sighed Miss Ciwle as I turned smoothly from Hucisko Street into the Jagiellonian Embankment, "I can see Instructor Uglymug hasn't wasted any time." "The bastard," I roared, "he's always in a sweat, he never talks about you except as…" "I know, I know," she wouldn't let me finish. "So what, if you've made progress – look how neatly we shift into fourth nowadays." And indeed, Mr Hrabal, I can only say those words of hers gave me wings – not just her words, but also the brush of her hand; that discreet, seemingly casual, perhaps truly accidental brush of her gentle fingers literally had the same effect on me as the breath of the Holy Spirit, the mysterious flurry of Paraclete's wings, so much so that I dashed past the station at almost a hundred and leaped onto Błędnik Bridge no slower; on the Great Avenue I went even faster, and in a single hop I was at the Opera.

"Please slow down at once," said Miss Ciwle, raising an eyebrow, "or we won't have a chance to chat. So your grandfather's next car was a Mercedes-Benz?" she asked, just as if our last conversation had only ended yesterday. "Was it really better than the *citron*?" "To be precise," I said, slowing down to sixty, "not his next, but his next few cars, because at the time Mercedes was the first company to introduce a one-year system, based on the idea that after twelve months you could take back a used car and, for a supplement of five hundred zlotys, drive a brand new car out of their garage." "Their garage?" wondered Miss Ciwle. "That's what it was called in those days," I said, not letting her interrupt, "because in those days the word 'salon' didn't refer to a hairdresser's, for example, a shoe shop or a laundry, like today; in that era a salon was still exclusively for various forms of social intercourse, making music, drinking wine, perhaps a game of bridge. So every year," I went on, "Grandfather Karol drove out of the Mercedes garage in a brand new car, but it was always exactly the same model, with the same moss-green body colour to boot, and if Grandfather was so very fond of the 170, it must have been because he was the undisputed winner of the fox hunt in it every single year." "Never," said Miss Ciwle, signalling that at the Kościuszko roundabout I should turn left into Słowacki Street, "now you're talking through your hat – fox hunting's an equestrian sport. How could you chase someone with a tied-on fox's brush across the fields and open ground on four wheels? It doesn't make sense, not even if the fox were motorised, and that's impossible anyway. What a lot of stories you must cook up! Please do it well so I can't feel it at all, clutch, change gear," she instructed me, "let's go up the hill in a lower gear!" As we zig-zagged up the moraine towards the airport a suburban scent of lilac and mown grass floated through the open car window, along with the cool shade of the beech woods, gloomy even in spring.

"I'm sorry," I said, "but you don't appreciate the inventiveness of the pre-war engineers. One day some balloon races were held in Mościce for the first time ever, no less than the national heats for the Gordon Bennett Cup, so when the engineers gathered at the club that evening, thrilled by the marvellous, fairytale sight of those spherical shapes in the sky, one of them came up with a revelation, the truly Wagnerian notion of combining their favourite sport of motoring, to which they were entirely devoted, with the sport of ballooning from now on. And in this simple way," I said, looking deep into Miss Ciwle's eyes, "the idea for a completely new kind of fox hunt was born, a revolutionary, democratic form of the sport, because after all," I calmly explained, "just like his colleagues, Grandfather Karol might be invited by Prince Sanguszko to go shooting, for instance, or even to the spring ball at Gumniska, but to be asked to go fox hunting on horseback was not so likely – that was in the realm of the

Almanach de Gotha; without at least seven batons on your crest, without sashes and maces, portraits too, in short, without high enough birth you were not *comme il faut*. So straightaway my grandfather and Engineer Krynicki devised the rules and regulations of the game, straightaway a collection was organised to cover all the costs of the races, above all to pay for the balloon, which was to be the fox. One spring morning less than two months later a vast, colourful sphere came into bloom on the green behind the factory, and at twenty-one minutes past ten local time it flew off into the ether. Steering it from the gondola hanging underneath was Mr Szuber from Sanok, who was an expert in aeronautics as well as being an ensign in an airborne regiment. So just imagine the excitement of the assembled motorists," I said, looking Miss Ciwle in the eyes again, "when half an hour later they were given the signal to jump into their cars and go their separate ways in search of the wind-driven sphere. But before they cranked up their starters, before the pilots unfolded the maps, first they tried to make visual contact through binoculars, because of course they needed to know in which direction the balloon was gliding, whether to go north after it to Szczucin, or the exact opposite, towards Zbylitowska Hill. So that was more or less the scene," I went on. "Mr Mierzejewski jumped into his enormous Packard, in which he usually transported eight children, Mr Nartowski slammed the door of his Hanza, Mr Hennel was ready to roll in his beautiful Tatra, Mr Kubiński was on the starting line, revving up his two-stroke DKW, and

One spring morning less than two months later a vast, colourful sphere came into bloom on the green behind the factory...

Jerzy Giorgiades, whom everyone took for an Armenian, but who was actually a Greek, was there to chase the balloon-fox in a fabulous Chevrolet, with Mr Jasilkowski in a Buick, whereas Engineer Hobbler drove a two-door BMW, as opposed to Engineer Wojnarski, who raced in a four-door Opel Olympia. Naturally, that wasn't all – here I should add Mr Zbigniew Krystek in his Opel Kapitän, Mr Żaba in his Fiat 504, Mr Mrowec in his Fiat 1100, Mr Krynicki in his Steyr, Mr Zachariewicz in his old Ford, and Mrs Kszyszkowska in her Adler Junior. And as for Mercedes-Benzes," I said as we drove out onto the plateau where at last I could change gear and accelerate, "there were three in Mościce; Dr Świerczyński and Engineer Śledziński both drove the same make as my grandfather, but both their models were two-door 170s, while Grandfather was steadfastly loyal to the four-door version. Motorcyclists entered the race as well, on Ariels, BMWs, Zundapps, BSAs, Victorias, Indianas and Harley-Davidsons."

"Not bad," said Miss Ciwle, interrupting this litany. "Please turn round at this forest road, because we're not going to the airport. By the way, it's practically impossible to interrupt you. So was that Mercedes really the best?" she asked, smiling so sweetly that I almost let go of the steering wheel. "You know, I don't mean the make, but that particular model – you said yourself how much it constantly needed doing to it every five hundred kilometres." "They were all like that in those days," I immediately cut in. "It was down to modern technology, not any specific make or model, so the

four-door 170 never failed to bring my grandfather good luck
in the races, helped, of course, by Grandmother Maria as the
pilot. For several evenings in a row before setting off on the
balloon hunt, my grandfather would listen to the weather
forecast on the radio, and go out onto the roof at night to
observe the sky and the clouds, the configuration of the
planets too. Then he'd sit over a map in his office, tracing the
balloon's probable trajectory in all possible directions and at
every likely wind speed. Finally he'd reckon it all up and jot it
down in his notebook in the form of tables and graphs, and
that must have been why he always succeeded in winning, he
always captured the trophy, because as soon as they'd taken
the balloon's bearings at the very start, Grandmother Maria
would glance at the tables and say: 'In three quarters of an
hour it'll be over Zakliczyn, route number thirteen, version
one, left at the second junction to Zgłobice.' So Grandfather
rushed straight for the goal by the shortest route, and if the
direction or speed of the wind changed abruptly he'd stop the
car for a moment, and there by the roadside, quick as
lightning, he'd set up an instrument he'd constructed himself,
a little windmill on an extendible pole; Grandmother would
take a precise reading from it and instantly enter the data into
the tables, then off they'd go in hot pursuit again, equipped
with a navigational variable that with the help of logarithms
and integrals infallibly determined the new position of the
balloon, and they always succeeded in catching up with the
airborne fox before the rest, wherever it had gone. Just

imagine what a beautiful scene – " by now we were at the
bottom of Słowacki Street, near the Prussian barracks –
"Grandfather Karol stops the Mercedes on the roadside verge
and runs across the meadow, to conform with the regulations
by getting as close as possible to the spot beneath the
gondola, then he takes out a bugle and plays a hunting call, at
the sound of which Ensign Aeronaut Szuber is immediately
obliged to cut short his flight by switching off the gas fire that
heats the air. By now they can see each other, now they're
waving at each other, and Ensign Szuber is throwing down the
anchor line with the fox's brush attached, my grandfather
grabs hold of it, and every single time it's the happiest
moment in his life. Now his wife is running across the
meadow towards him, and they hug each other, they kiss, sing
and dance. Ensign Szuber takes the regulation bottle of
champagne and three crystal glasses from a wooden box, and
they drink to their victory, while other cars and motorbikes
start coming down the road. It must have been a really
fantastic feeling to win that sort of race," I finished my tale at
the roundabout where Grunwaldzka Avenue meets
Kościuszko Street, "when you consider that according to their
regulations only one competitor and his pilot could triumph –
there was no second or third place, just like hunting on
horseback, where only one rider tears off the brush and rakes
in all the honour, and he's the rightful, one and only king
when everyone drinks his health at the club that evening."
"Was the prize a big one?" asked Miss Ciwle, taking a roll-up

from her silver cigarette case and lighting it with the car lighter. "Was it bigger than the reward given to engine driver Hnatiuk for ramming the Citroën?" "What on earth do you mean?" I said, moving smoothly into the middle lane. "Mr Hnatiuk didn't get his reward for destroying anything but for promoting the locomotives made at Chrzanów. As far as I remember he got one thousand five hundred zlotys, a lot for those days, considering a Polish Fiat cost around five thousand then, and a gold Omega on top engraved with a dedication: *To a Hero of the Polish State Railways from the Management*. So no, the prize for winning the race was purely honorary – it was a bronze badge shaped like a fox, inscribed *Mościce Balloon Hunt*, with the date; what's more the winner always stood the first three rounds at the club, so from the empirical side of things, on top of the honour and glamour of winning he had to pay extra." "Not like nowadays," sighed Miss Ciwle, "these days people try to make money out of anything at all – it's reached a point where if they could sell their own shit no one would be put off by the stink." "Now you're exaggerating, surely," I cried. "It's true dialectical materialism has changed into materialism of the practical kind, but is that a reason to see it all that way?" "You don't know what I'm talking about," she said, taking another drag at her roll-up and blowing out a thin stream of acrid smoke. "Have you ever heard of Doctor Elephant?"

Moments later, when I had answered in the negative, in a subdued tone Miss Ciwle began her tale, and I can tell you, my

dear Mr Hrabal, shivers went down my spine at the thought
that had I been ill like Jarek, I too could have ended up in the
clutches of Doctor Elephant, who was indeed an expert at
removing aneurisms from the brain, but was even better at
reducing his patients to ruin by demanding bribes, firstly for a
hospital bed, then for endless consultations, and finally for the
operation itself, which he went through with even when it was
a foregone conclusion and he knew perfectly well the patient
was bound to die, and even in cases where the operation
wasn't necessary; for Doctor Elephant was a past master at
making money disappear and always knew how to squeeze it
out of desperate people, who to save their loved ones were
willing to sell literally everything and get into debt too. Such
was the case of Jarek and his sister: first of all, to get a place at
the clinic and pay for the operation they had sold their flat,
then it turned out the diagnosis was wrong, there would be no
operation, the illness was atypical, requiring further, long-
term treatment, so at that point Miss Ciwle had made her way
into Doctor Elephant's consulting room and demanded her
money back, at least the cost of the operation, at which Doctor
Elephant had coldly declared that he would call the police at
once and have her prosecuted, because this was provocation,
it was an outrage, how dare she accuse him of fraud right
there, in his own consulting room – where, when and who had
seen her give him such a large sum of money? "The son of a
bitch just threw me out," said Miss Ciwle with tears in her
eyes. "The flat our parents left us has gone to the devil, Jarek

was immediately discharged from hospital, and in no time at all I had to turn the allotment shed into something habitable for the winter, because otherwise we'd have had to sleep at the station, and it's pure luck that our parents left us that worker's allotment too. I can assure you," she said, stubbing out her cigarette in the ashtray lid, "our case isn't at all exceptional, and now I'm taking Jarek to various miracle-workers, who even if they can't cure him at least won't rob us, because they never take more than for a visit to the dentist, and besides they pay for their own consulting rooms and some sort of taxes, unlike Doctor Elephant whose research, consulting room and equipment we suckers finance out of our own purses." "It's outrageous," I cried. "Can't someone catch him out?" "How could they?" said Miss Ciwle, wiping her nose on her handkerchief. "Let's change the subject – did your grandfather's Mercedes have overhead or side valves?"

My dear Mr Hrabal, I think you'll understand that after what I'd heard, stories of old cars and the jolly motoring enjoyed by some gentlemen engineers seemed trivial and totally incongruous, on top of which we were just going past that big white building on the corner of Horseback Way and Curie-Skłodowska Street that belongs to the Medical Academy, the building where in the days of the Akademie der Praktischen Medizin in Danzig Professor Spanner used to make soap out of human remains, and I started feeling sick as I remembered those photographs and witness statements Zofia Nałkowska described in her diary just after the war, hot

news, as it were, because the left-over ashes were still
smoking at the time in the handy crematorium next door,
where roasted human torsos and strips of torn-off skin were
still lying in the boilers; I felt sick when I realised that the
spirit of that German "Academy of Practical Medicine" was
still present within the walls of the Medical Academy, if
people like Doctor Elephant were universally respected there,
shaken by the hand, congratulated on their thesis defence,
wished all the best on their name day, sent letters full of
deference and awarded rector's prizes, all despite everyone
knowing about their methods. "I hope," I said, patting Miss
Ciwle on the knee, "he rots in hell." "Hell," she laughed
incredulously. "People like him are insured in every possible
way. You know what, Doctor Elephant performs every tenth
operation for free – he calls it 'Saint Anthony's fund'. Maybe
he really does hope it'll help him, though I think if you add up
all those cases of infanticide, people like him must end up in
hell." "Infanticide?" I cut in abruptly. "You don't mean to say
that bloody doctor is a gynaecologist too, using ultra-modern
tubes and pumps to suck those jelly-like little creatures out of
their mothers' wombs and straight down the sink, do you?"
"You what?" said Miss Ciwle indignantly. "I never said that,
but you should know Doctor Elephant is an expert procrasti-
nator – if an operation is needed he waits until the parents
have collected the whole sum, and I probably don't have to tell
you that quite often the waiting goes on a bit too long and the
little patient dies. That's why they call him Doctor Mengele,

the angel of death, though I'd rather call him a doctor of economic law, because ultimately it's not nationality or denomination that decides if someone has a chance of survival, but money, purely and simply cash..."

My dear Mr Hrabal, there was a very long silence; now we were driving slowly along Horseback Way, down the avenue of old lime trees that were planted here over two hundred years ago at the expense of Daniel Gralath, and it occurred to me that if only Spanner and Elephant had been fond of freemasonry like Mayor Gralath they might never have disgraced their medical vocation, remaining loyal to Hippocrates instead, because the spirit of freemasonry calls for self-sacrifice and brotherhood and forbids one from thinking of one's fellow man purely in terms of bars of soap or nine-figure sums in one's bank account. But then again that same Masonic spirit vanished from this city long ago, as the name of the road we were driving down shows, for example: first it was called Hauptallee, then Hindenburg, then Hitler, after that Rokossowski, and finally Victory, just as if all the successive rulers of this city were afraid of Gralath, if only of his memory. I'm sure that was the case, because the Nazi parades used to march along this avenue between the ancient lime trees from the Opera to the Town Centre, and so did the May Day processions from the Town Centre to the Opera; somewhere within the invisible current of time, all those brass bands, swastikas, hammers and sickles got mixed up together, while Doctor Spanner and Doctor Elephant watched it all from the windows of the Institute of Practical Anatomy, clasping each other warmly by the hand, for if after the thesis of the torchlight parades the antithesis of the communist marches had come and gone, finally for people like them the moment of synthesis had arrived, the era of unimpeded creative activity and the arithmetic of pure profit, washed clean of all the stains of nowadays superfluous ideals. "Yes, yes, my friend, congratulations," said Spanner with tears in his eyes, "you've lived to see some fine times – the doctors at this school have never had such opportunities before." "But my dear fellow, please don't exaggerate," said Elephant, politely shaking his head. "Your contribution to the post-war growth of the cosmetics industry is just as worthy of admiration and envy, especially as you had to start from almost zero on the other side of the ocean."

"What are you thinking about?" asked Miss Ciwle, breaking the silence in the little Fiat. "About the guy who as Mayor spent a hundred thousand out of his own pocket to build and beautify this road," I said. "Impossible," exclaimed Miss Ciwle. "That's too good to be true. Out of his own pocket, not the city's coffers, you said? There hasn't been anything about it on TV, or how he wrote it off his tax. That Balcerowicz is a racketeer, isn't he? He'd never let anyone get away with it." "Yes," I smiled at Miss Ciwle, "but in those days the tax laws were completely different, and when Daniel Gralath wrote down his bequest in his will, setting aside a hundred thousand guldens for cultivating this piece of land and laying out this avenue, as well as for buying and planting several thousand lime trees, there was no Balcerowicz around and that's why the avenue is so long and wide. Just take a look – it's the only place in Gdańsk where to this day there aren't any traffic jams, it's the city's one single monument to some truly creative thinking." "What does 'in those days' mean?" asked Miss Ciwle. "What year was it, and who was this Gralath chap?" "I told you, he was the mayor of our city, and on occasion Master of the Royal Hunt. He published the first bibliography of works on electricity," I said, moving into the right-hand lane and turning right at People's Assembly Square towards Gradowa Hill, "and he also went in for the secret sciences of the Rosicrucians. He was strongly suspected of belonging to a Masonic lodge, but no one ever managed to confirm it – not so in the case of his son, also called Daniel; after studying under Immanuel Kant himself, Daniel the younger founded a lodge in Gdańsk called the Two Crowned Lions, in whose library collection many books belonging to Gralath the elder were found, most of them on the rituals of initiation, and that's why people thought Gralath the elder must have been a freemason too, which gives us the obvious explanation why under no single authority, whether it was the Prussians, the Nazis, the Poles, the communists or the Soviets, has this fine avenue ever been named after its magnanimous sponsor, who made the bequest in his will shortly before his death in the year 1767 to be precise."

"Jesus, please turn into the petrol station," cried Miss Ciwle, "we're out of fuel! I've been listening to you as if you'd just got back from paradise, instead of looking at the petrol gauge! Left here, let's fill her up – you forgot the indicator, as usual!" My dear Mr Hrabal, that business with the indicator was our running sore, like a refrain in every lesson; it's not true that I forgot to indicate, not at all, I never once forgot, but as you'll admit yourself, what was the point of indicating at the training ground, for instance, where apart from us there was no other car, bike or pedestrian, or on a road like that one by the petrol station, when nothing was coming either down the hill from the cemetery or up it from People's Assembly Square? It'd be like operating a lighthouse in broad daylight, i.e. completely unnecessary, but Miss Ciwle was of a different opinion and in this situation she never failed to say in a rather offended tone: "Mr H., we even indicate in the wilderness," and at that moment I always felt as if life was turning another of its circles, because I remembered your driving lessons on the Java motorbike and wondered if, as you turned from Wenceslas Square, let's say into Krakovska Street, the instructor reminded you: "Please put your arm out to the right," because in those days motorbikes weren't yet fitted with indicator lights, and I'm sure driving with only one hand on the handlebars must have cost you a nervous moment, not to mention the instructor. So right then, just by the petrol station and the cemetery, Miss Ciwle made her ritual remark: "Mr H., we even indicate in the wilderness," but on this occasion I hadn't time to think of you or to reply with my equally ritual comment: "Then let's go to Greenland," because just before turning left her little Fiat coughed, hiccupped and backfired before coming to a decisive halt, so we had to jump out and push it the last few metres steeply uphill, then turn left, and as soon as it began to roll downwards onto the petrol station forecourt, we had to jump back in from either side at the very same moment and free-wheel down to the petrol pump, which we managed to do with surprisingly symmetrical precision, as if we were a pair of figure-skating dancers.

"Please would you fill her up," said Miss Ciwle, briefly struggling with the petrol cap key. "I'll go and pay." And she set off for the cash desk; meanwhile, my dear Mr Hrabal, holding the hose and bending low over the little Fiat's fuel intake, I turned my head like Lot's wife to admire Miss Ciwle's incredibly graceful walk, her beautiful bearing that had nothing tacky about it, nothing of the porn film, none of the atmosphere of a peep show booth – no, Miss Ciwle simply floated to the cash desk like the hind in the Song of Songs. I tell you, dear Mr Hrabal, those black jeans of hers, her dark silk blouse, her pumps, leather waistcoat and silver earrings glinting among the waves of her loose, coppery-chestnut hair, all this reflected in the petrol station windows multiplied the incredible effect of sheer beauty floating on the violet-tinted spring twilight, but my reverie was soon cut short when Miss Ciwle came running out of the petrol station, looking upset. "Bloody hell!" she cried, "please stop pumping, I forgot to bring any cash, and they're refusing to take the registration document as security because they've already got three drawers full of them. You sit in the car and I'll nip home, it's not far from here." "No need for you to run up the hill," I said, hanging up the hose, "I'll pay."

Shortly after we were back in the Fiat. "Can we go somewhere, to the seaside perhaps?" said Miss Ciwle, hesitating for a moment before saying more. "You know, I've got this thing where whenever I'm down in the dumps I get in the car and spend the evening just driving ahead, wherever. Sometimes I've just got to get out of the house with no partic- ular aim in mind, so let's go, and please tell me another story, I've got very fond of that. Has the story of your grandparents and their cars been published yet? I'd love to read it. Maybe you've got a copy? Jarek would be pleased as punch." "No," I said, moving slowly down the hill towards May the Third Street, "and I've never even thought I could write about it." "Could?" she said, giving me an inquiring look. "Should, you mean – it's fantastic, the level crossing and the *citron*, or the wall at the prince's palace. But what I'd like to read about best is the balloon racing, the fox hunt and the motoring club." "What more can I say?" I said, turning onto Błędnik Bridge with the indicator on. "The very last hunt took place not in spring, but in August 1939. Just as ever Grandfather Karol made meticulous preparations for it, and just as ever Grandmother Maria accompanied him as his pilot with the map-case on her lap, but this time the balloon, or rather the weather, played tricks on them all. It was a fine day and the birds were hopping about in the stubble fields, but the air had

been hot throughout the torrid summer, and not a single puff
of wind was willing to emerge from Boreas's sack. The balloon
moved slowly towards the River Dunajec and hung above it in
mid-stream; some of the drivers started taking the ferry across
to Wierzchosławice, counting on the fact that eventually it
would fly in that direction, while others, not believing in such
a turn of events, waited on this bank. But though no one could
feel the slightest shiver of wind, as if in the grip of an invisible
hand the balloon began to move south, right upstream; to be
more precise, it was moving along the exact course of the
river, following the very middle of its rapid stream – it looked
just as if Tritons were pulling it along on strings, heading for
the source. So this time the hunt was rather unusual, with
cars and motorbikes proceeding up the Dunajec along both its
banks like a guard of honour, and everyone appeared to have
an even chance, at least until the second a gust of wind pushed
the balloon towards the left or right bank. So as some of the
competitors drove slowly through Wojnicz, Melsztyn, Czchów
and Lower Łososina, no less numerous a retinue was
advancing through Zgłobice, Zakliczyn and Rożnów all the
way to Gródek – not Gródek Jagielloński, the one near Lwów,
but Gródek on the Dunajec of course." "So what side was your
grandfather's Mercedes on?" asked Miss Ciwle. "Good
question," I said, slowing down a bit on the cobbles on
Siennicki Bridge, from where we could see the mighty hulls of
ships and the tugboats at the illuminated wharves.
"Grandfather and Grandmother drove through Rożnów and

Gródek, that is, along the right bank, so to speak. 'Somehow I think it's going to fly our way, Maria,' Grandfather kept saying, rolling a long since burnt-out cigar between finger and thumb. 'I'm not at all sure of that, Karol,' replied my grandmother, 'I'm afraid it might just as well fly their way and land somewhere near Limanowa, and then' – she glanced at the map – 'we definitely won't win, because our nearest crossing is either at Nowy Sącz, or else we'll have to go back to Czchów.' And just imagine," I said as we drove along the Dead Vistula into Stogi, "the balloon stopped almost at the very end of Rożnów Lake, exactly mid-way between Tęgoborz on the left bank of the river and Zbyszyce on the right, and there it hung in the air without moving for a good half hour. So the competitors started getting out of their cars, parked their motorbikes and took out their food hampers, and a veritable picnic was soon underway. Only my grandfather didn't take part in it – he never got out of the Mercedes, on the roof of which Grandmother Maria had set up that special device of theirs for measuring the speed and direction of the wind, their little windmill on a pole with a rotary meter and a tiny barometer. 'Something flickered,' whispered Maria at last, 'not much, but in our direction.' 'Fold it up and get in,' whispered Grandfather in reply, and just imagine," I said, as we drove through the pine woods along the tram line and the dunes that led to the beach, "as they drove back down the road to Gródek the picnicking ladies and gentlemen stared after them in astonishment, but not for long, because as soon

...the balloon stopped almost at the very end of Rożnów Lake ... and there it hung in the air without moving for a good half hour. So the competitors started getting out of their cars, parked their motorbikes and took out their food hampers, and a veritable picnic was soon underway.

as a stronger gust of wind shifted the balloon their way, they all leapt up from the grass, started their vehicles and dashed after my grandparents' Mercedes, which literally a couple of hundred metres beyond Zbyszyce had turned into the road to Korzenna, that is eastwards, because that was the direction where the wind was rising by the minute. 'Grybów or Ciężkowice?' asked Grandfather, as at a giddy speed of sixty-five kilometres per hour they flashed past the last houses in Wojnarowa. 'Better Ciężkowice, turn left in a bit,' replied Grandmother Maria, and she wasn't wrong, because just then the balloon appeared some three hundred metres ahead of the car's bonnet, now moving quite quickly in exactly the direction indicated. But this time they weren't fated to win the race."

I parked the Fiat by the tram loop and we set off down the path towards the beach. "Nor was anyone else, because as the balloon was gliding over Bobowa a blast of anti-aircraft fire came thundering from behind a small hill above the River Biała, and little grey clouds burst into bloom all round the colourful canopy and the gondola, until finally one of the bullets pierced the envelope and the balloon dropped into the meadow like a great big parachute. Ensign Szuber was immediately surrounded and arrested by a detachment of the Border Guard Corps, and there was an awful fuss, because he wasn't carrying a licence or any identity papers, but he did have a camera and was taken for a German spy. Grandfather Karol ran to his aid, but his arguments were of no use at all,

nor were those of the next competitors to arrive. Their
explanation that the balloon was registered and duly marked
'SP-ALP Mościce' was no use either, nor were the guarantees
of all the gentlemen engineers and mechanics as a group.
Captain Rymwid Ostoja-Kończypolski was implacable and
ordered the entire assembly to proceed under escort to Mrs
Klungman's restaurant to wait there for further develop-
ments. So that was the final flight of the SP-ALP Mościce
balloon and the final fox hunt: at Mrs Klungman's restaurant
they were served quails, roast veal, chops, carp Jewish-style,
Ukrainian beetroot soup, Russian piroshki, goose liver, fried
barbel, pickled mushrooms, stuffed duck, pork with plums,
shoulder of pork, ribs, consommé, boiled beef, and all this
with assorted vegetables and salads, as well as Okocim beer,
Żywiec beer, Czech Pilsner, five kinds of Baczewski vodka,
French brandy and champagne, and Hungarian wines from Mr
Lippoczy's stores, followed by hot chocolate, pistachio-
flavoured ice cream, grapes, cream cakes, éclairs, Pischinger
torte and plum cake, coffee, tea, Sinalco, raspberry juice and
lemonade, and all at moderate prices without a holiday resort
visitor's tax, for where on earth was Bobowa compared with
Iwonicz, Truskawiec or Krynica?" "Jesus, my stomach's
rumbling!" laughed Miss Ciwle, sitting on the sand. "I
wouldn't mind being under that sort of arrest, as long as I had
some cash on me. Were they held there for long?" "About
three hours," I said, sitting down beside her, "but Ensign
Szuber was in a much worse situation because he was taken to

the Border Guard Corps' field HQ for interrogation and got nothing but a glass of water. Meanwhile at the restaurant they had a ball beneath the fox's brush, which Grandfather Karol had hung up from the ceiling rafters. Toast after toast was raised to next year's race and its triumphant winner, since this year's had been a damp squib, but many of them must already have known deep down that they were drinking on credit at the highest risk and interest rate, that they were signing a bill of exchange with no deadline, which could become valueless at any moment. Grandfather Karol sensed it perfectly as he kept filling Grandmother Maria's wineglass, which annoyed her because she didn't like feeling tipsy, but Grandfather knew what he was doing. He leaned over her and said in a hushed tone: 'Maria, we're never going to be happier than this again, we must capture this moment like a fly in amber, perhaps even preserve it for our grandchildren.' 'Why leap to our grandchildren?' she asked in amazement. 'Even if there's a war the world will go back to normal – it always does, doesn't it?' she said, giving him a trustful look. 'A quart of wheat for a denarius,' said Grandfather, smiling bitterly. 'What denarius? What are you on about?' said Grandmother, discreetly placing a hand on his wineglass and moving it her way. And they simply couldn't get through to each other," I explained to Miss Ciwle. "They couldn't, because during the other, the first world war, they'd had completely different experiences. She spent almost all of it in Switzerland, while he was in the trenches; she was busy organising aid committees, while he was studying new types of cannon and shells; she was writing letters, while he was adding the details to artillery maps, and afterwards, once they were back home in Lwów and could finally breathe easy, yet another war broke out, not on a world scale this time, but between Poland and Ukraine, so he had to go and fire guns again, while she organised more aid committees. So you see, they had completely different vantage points, and not for the last time either, because almost as soon as the Ukrainian war was over, the Bolsheviks marched on Poland. This time Grandfather was assigned to an armoured train, and although he just sat comfortably in a steel turret marked 'Courageous', he still had to fire guns again, not into the air this time." "Just a moment," said Miss Ciwle, lighting a roll-up, "do you mean to say that while fighting for Lwów against the Ukrainians your grandfather just fired into the air, like a sort of Schweik?" "I don't know that he did," I replied, "but that's what he always used to say, because the war against the Ukrainians was his greatest source of woe. 'We're going to win,' he said at the time, 'but how are we going to live together in the same city afterwards, how can we look each other in the eye?' As for the Bolsheviks," I went on, "you can be sure the guns on the 'Courageous' armoured train didn't fire into the Lord God's window, but at Budyonny's galloping cavalry – Grandfather must have thought of them there, at the restaurant near Bobowa in August 1939, he must surely have remembered those horsemen of the Apocalypse swarming along. Anyway," I concluded, "he had no illusions that the

...Grandfather was assigned to an armoured train, and although he just sat comfortably in a steel turret marked 'Courageous', he still had to fire guns again, not into the air this time.
(Inside the armoured train – Grandfather Karol is first on the right)

approaching war would be like the previous ones and maybe that's why, once they were back in the Mercedes, he quietly repeated that quote from Saint John about the quart of wheat and the denarius, which upset Grandmother, who thought he had drunk a drop too much and should let her take the wheel, which naturally he refused to agree to. So they spent that last drive home together from the fox hunt under the black cloud of a silent quarrel. They slowly passed the house of an illustrious tzaddik, where a crowd of Hassidim had gathered, then drove on full headlights down a winding road through hills plunged in darkness; the engine kept up a steady hum, while an incessant cricket concerto sounded through the open window, and they never forgot the unusual atmosphere of that August night, because it was true," I said, gently putting my arm round Miss Ciwle, "they were never so happy again."

And just imagine, my dear Mr Hrabal, once I'd completed that final sentence she put her hand on my arm, and there we sat without moving, like a couple of school-children in love, staring into the dark blue mantle of the bay, as the lights of ships slowly moved across it, some of them standing in the roadstead, others on their way to Kaliningrad, Stockholm, Helsinki, Visby and Hilversum or wherever else. At that moment we could feel an uncanny atmosphere, a sort of psychic Gulf Stream flowing between us, not because of our innocent physical contact, but for extremely basic reasons, fundamental, so to say: quite simply, my dear Mr Hrabal, we could sense that we were fraternal souls, something Shelley, Keats, Byron and Mickiewicz wrote about, something everyone laughs at nowadays, scholars and artists included, something priests aren't aware of and writers don't know about any more – in short, we were united by that long lost language, like a gossamer thread, though it wasn't autumn yet, but a night in May; Arcturus was reigning supreme in the sky, along with the equally bright Spica in the constellation of Virgo, while the Great Bear went rolling by from the direction of Bornholm towards Hel, as our feet were lapped by the waves of the sea, still chilly at this time of year.

"That's really beautiful," whispered Miss Ciwle. "The Mercedes gliding along in the dark, and those crickets – do finish the story, do tell me what came next." "The German planes," I replied, "that Captain Rymwid Ostoja-Kończypolski's batteries failed to hit, the German tanks that the cavalry detachments failed to halt – in a word, what came next was catastrophe. But before it all happened, a few days before the outbreak of war my grandfather managed to take one more photograph and hand the roll of film to Mr Chaskiel Bronstein, and that was the last picture he ever took in pre-war Poland – a family portrait: on the left, at the edge of the road stood Grandmother Maria, then the two lads, i.e. my uncle and my father, and Grandfather, who couldn't be in the frame of course, but who also appeared in the picture in the form of a distinct shadow. I tell you, every time I look at that photo, every time I touch that small, yellowing piece of card

*... and that was the last picture he ever took in pre-war Poland –
a family portrait: on the left, at the edge of the road stood Grandmother
Maria, then the two lads, i.e. my uncle and my father, and Grandfather,
who couldn't be in the frame of course, but who also appeared in the
picture in the form of a distinct shadow.*

from Mr Bronstein's shop, I feel a surge of emotion, because that shadow was like an omen of things to come, it was like Grandfather's silent absence for the next few years. And as for the Mercedes," I said, pre-empting Miss Ciwle's question, "that was also the farewell photograph." "Yes," she interrupted me, "the Germans must have requisitioned it." "Not at all," I explained, "once the bombs had started falling Grandfather received instructions for all documents containing secrets of chemical technology to be taken east, where they would be safe, because everyone assumed that the front would hold on the River Dunajec or at worst on the San, and would remain there until the relief troops arrived from France, but that was wishful thinking. As the Mercedes ploughed its way along roads full of refugees on whom the Luftwaffe pilots had already been testing their skills, he was sure he would never complete this task, and that he'd never get to Lwów in time, where an Intelligence Department agent was supposed to be waiting for him at the Hotel Georges, but things turned out quite differently. About twenty kilometres outside Lwów he caught sight of a Red Army cavalry detachment ahead of him, a reconnaissance party, and wanted to turn around at once, because of the two evils facing him he thought it would be better to hide and complete his mission somewhere on the German side of the line. But it was already too late, the Red Army men spurred on their horses and surrounded the Mercedes, while their commanding officer, a lieutenant with a pockmarked face, all but clapped his hands with joy at the sight of the car. 'We're in luck today all right, the commissar will be delighted,' he said to his men, and shouted at my grandfather in Russian: 'Get out, you swine!' So just imagine," I told Miss Ciwle over the steady roar of the waves, "that lieutenant wrote out a requisition receipt and said: 'Here's a document for the Polak so he won't go round telling tales about our army stealing,' then smiled and clapped my grandfather on the shoulder, saying: 'We know what your hostile propaganda is like.' So there stood my grandfather before that pockmarked lieutenant and silently accepted the requisition receipt, while the soldiers ransacked the car and, to my grandfather's amazement, threw everything they didn't need into the ditch: a Bosch spanner set in an ebonite box went flying into a clump of burdock, followed by Grandfather's moth-eaten dust-coat, a pair of galoshes, an oilcan, an empty goggles case, and also a bundle of documents tied with a paper string; luckily they didn't look through them after removing them from the leather briefcase, which they kept, of course. And all this took no more than seven minutes," I explained to Miss Ciwle. "As soon as they had set off back to Lwów, Grandfather lit a cigarette and stared after the clouds of dust billowing from under the hoofs of the lieutenant's riderless horse, which now ran freely behind the Mercedes while its master freely changed the gears, switched on the indicators and tried out the horn; meanwhile the soldiers escorting the car fired into the air and sang a fine, catchy song about how the Polish gentlemen will never forget those wild dogs, the

Cossacks. Only when they had disappeared around the bend did Grandfather jump down into the ditch and recover his things, then he slowly started walking towards Lwów in the hope that in spite of the unexpected Soviet occupation he might yet manage to complete his mission. And that's how I imagine him on that road: walking along slowly in his old dust-coat, stopping now and then as the ebonite toolbox is very heavy, and in the other hand, or rather under his arm, he's holding the sheaf of secret documents from the National Nitro-Compound Factory in Mościce tied with a paper string, which the Intelligence Department agent would be waiting to receive from him at the Hotel Georges."

My instructress's pretty little feet, bathed like mine in the chill waves of the Baltic, vanished from time to time beneath the wet sand; absorbed in this childish game of burying and uncovering her own extremities from the amorphous grey mass Miss Ciwle seemed not to be listening to my story, but as soon as I fell silent after mentioning the intelligence agent, she immediately asked: "So did they meet at that hotel?" "The Hotel Georges," I went on, "was already full of Soviet officers and the entire dining hall was like military headquarters once the war is over and won. Grandfather went there by tram from Ujejski Street where earlier he had changed his clothes and rested. So he didn't go into the hotel, he just stood on the pavement and stared in the windows of the dazzlingly illuminated hall as if he were a passer-by, and he couldn't believe his own eyes: waiters young and old, pageboys and clerks, literally everyone was dancing attendance at the tables, serving the Soviet officers with beef stew, joints of roast meat, mutton, Hungarian wine, French cognac and Baczewski vodka, and they were paying most obligingly with some strange bits of paper. Grandfather stood on tiptoes and with his face pressed against the window he saw that they were Red Army requisition receipts, just like the one he'd been given for the Mercedes. It was an extraordinary sight: the high-spirited officers had smashed all the wineglasses and had nothing to drink out of but tumblers, as if fully aware that in a few hours the hotel cellar would be completely empty, for who was going to provide a new delivery of Tokay, absinthe, Armagnac or Bordeaux? So they were pulling entire booklets of requisition receipts from their pockets and pressing them onto the silver salvers, while the waiters smiled and thanked them for such colossal tips, as if they realised that the Red Army officers were just as capable of paying for all this loathsome, bourgeois luxury with lead shot rather than ration cards.

"Grandfather stepped back from the window and walked towards Hetman's Embankment, feeling crushed and downcast, not so much by the sudden occupation and the loss of the Mercedes – after all, in Central Europe such events are nothing out of the ordinary, being as it were the natural outward state of affairs – but by the fact that this dark and ominous force had unexpectedly invaded a sphere that had never been subject to annexation or incursion before, and so had seemed safest of all; it was that the entire machine of war

was gradually but systematically encroaching on the sphere of
his memory, destroying its delicate tissue bit by bit, sapping
the strength of the pure, sharp images, ripping up the past and
imposing its own particular filter on it, not yet familiar to the
nations of Central Europe, not quite like anything else. As he
marched along Hetman's Embankment Grandfather
intuitively understood this; he realised that all his memories
of the Hotel Georges and of Mariacki Square, all the times he
had met his fiancée, friends or colleagues there, would now be
completely different, filled for ever with the singing and toasts
of the Soviet officers, their cigarette smoke, the pungent smell
of eau-de-Cologne and sweat, the noise of the accordion and
glass crunching under their boots; if he were ever to think of
the conversation he'd had with his fiancée when she'd told
him about her Hungarian mother, for instance, who died so
young and so tragically, and he had told her the lengthy story
of his great-great-grandfather, a doctor in the Napoleonic
army who was a great brawler and carouser, even if he were to
summon up every single ingredient of their meeting, so many
years ago, including the clouds above the square, the clatter of
horse-drawn vehicles, the tram bells and the rays of sunlight
falling onto their table through the restaurant window, a row
of sweaty, purple faces would never fail to superimpose itself
on that image, the rims of their caps lying on the tablecloths,
or the wads of requisition receipts they kept pressing on the
waiters, and I'll admit," I went on tirelessly as Miss Ciwle
withdrew her feet from the water, "such thoughts were not

comforting in a city where almost all the streets were already hung with red banners saying: *Glory to the Liberators of Western Ukraine, Down with the Bourgeoisie, The Working Classes are with Stalin* – and as if that were not enough, somewhere near the Sobieski monument Grandfather noticed a Mercedes-Benz speeding down the far side of the avenue, a four-door 170 with moss-green bodywork, and recognised his car, or rather the car that had had a radical change of owner.

"Just then he heard a voice behind him say, 'Engineer? Please don't turn round, let's walk along side by side, nice and normal. Yes, lucky you didn't go into the hotel – it's swarming with agents, but if you had our man would have intercepted you and taken you out through the kitchen. Yes, it's all rather complicated but we're in control of the situation, naturally. Better not stare after that Mercedes or you'll attract attention. I'll tell you who's riding in it – that's Commissar Khrushchev, we'll be hearing plenty more about him, but *à propos*, have you got the papers with you?' They took the tram to Ujejski Street," I said, taking Miss Ciwle by the arm as we strolled down from the beach, "where in Grandmother Maria's old flat they drank a whole bottle of absinthe, so no wonder their conversation at first centred on the Baczewski vodka and liqueur factory, bombed by the Luftwaffe a few days earlier. 'It burned down on the ninth of September,' the intelligence agent dryly reported. 'And this morning the Soviets arrested both Mr Baczewskis, Stefan and Adam.' 'Was it to hand them some requisition receipts?' wondered Grandfather. 'It's called

getting rid of alien elements,' explained the agent. 'Why don't
you escape to Hungary with me, and on to France? In a year
we can return to Warsaw via defeated Berlin.' 'What about
this lot?' said Grandfather, nodding towards the open window,
where outside a tank was rumbling by. 'France and Britain
won't stand for this annexation,' said the intelligence ace, 'and
what's more we'll appeal to the League of Nations.' But
somehow" – by now Miss Ciwle and I were getting back into
the little Fiat – "my grandfather had no faith in the Allies, nor
did he put his trust in the League of Nations, so next day he
set off back to Mościce over the brand new border, which
hadn't even been ploughed up by the Germans and Soviets
yet. When he got home at last, instead of reporting for work at
the now German factory, he spent days on end looking
through old photographs, putting his archive in order, writing
the missing dates and names of people and places on their
cardboard backing. As he unrolled it again, this particular reel
of time already felt like something very different from a
catalogue of ordinary memories; it felt as if those moments
captured in the past by the cold shutter of his Leica now made
up a completely new volume that he'd never intended to
create, consisting of chance moments, twists and turns of
light, bits and pieces of matter and voices that stopped
sounding long ago; it was like a suddenly open, secret gate,
revealing a previously unknown vista to the astonished
passer-by, a wonderful spectacle of phantoms of time and
space, swirling like golden pillars of dust in a dark old granary.

...Grandfather ... spent days on end looking through old photographs, putting his archive in order, writing the missing dates and names of people and places on their cardboard backing. As he unrolled it again, this partic- ular reel of time already felt like something very different from a catalogue of ordinary memories; it felt as if those moments captured in the past by the cold shutter of his Leica now made up a completely new volume.
(The author's father leaning on a Citroën)

That's why Grandfather felt an urge to see Mr Bronstein," I said, as we drove back over Siennicki Bridge, crossing the lifeless ribbon of the port canal, where the hulls of the ships looked like the slumbering bodies of exotic monsters; "in order," I continued, "to share that perception with him and to buy some spare film, because every day since the Germans had invaded, something else had been banned, and Grandfather was afraid the Poles would soon be forbidden to take photographs too, just like listening to the radio, skiing and symphony concerts, not to mention studying geology at public lectures run by the Natural History Society, which, like all societies and colleges, had simply been closed down.

"So he cycled to Tarnów to buy Gevaert film and photographic paper from Mr Bronstein, but the shop was already closed; as someone was still quietly bustling about behind the scenes, Grandfather went into the back yard and knocked gently three times. 'Engineer,' said Mr Bronstein gladly, 'I heard you'd been arrested by the Soviets in Lwów – so it's not true.' He offered his guest a chair. 'This time,' replied Grandfather, 'I only paid with the car, but I didn't wait for a next time, I came home instead.' 'It's no better here,' said Mr Bronstein, pointing to his armband with the star on it. 'I'm closing the shop and leaving for Argentina.' 'Argentina?' asked Grandfather in amazement, 'how?' 'Don't ask how, please just pray that I can get my family out. I bought the passport two weeks before the war broke out, but it's only in my name, and they have to go to the ghetto; they've taken our

flat away – you can't begin to imagine what sort of bribes I had
to pay at our community office to guarantee them at least a
room with a stove, but they'll manage to sit it out. At least
they won't throw you out of the factory. Please accept this
from me for old time's sake.' Mr Bronstein handed
Grandfather several boxes of photographic paper and a dozen
rolls of Gevaert film; when he tried to insist on paying, the
photographer was affronted and firmly said he wouldn't
accept any money from such a good customer this time – his
best customer in the whole city; even when the nationalists
had scrawled the words 'Don't go to the Jew' across his
window, Grandfather had ostentatiously parked his Mercedes
in front of the shop and gone inside, then bought far more
than he needed. Once they had warmly bid each other
farewell, in parting Grandfather simply added: 'You know
what, I'm not going to the factory any more, the Germans can
shift for themselves,' and went out into the yard, but his
bicycle was gone; someone had stolen it just like that. So
Grandfather walked down Krakowska Street, past the German
gendarme patrols, and wondered what would happen next,
since the French had not launched an offensive, nor had the
British dropped a single bomb on Berlin, though meanwhile
the Germans and Soviets were staging joint march-pasts. At
this point he remembered how a few years ago he had founded
a small firm importing chemicals in the Free City of Danzig,
how he'd been harassed by inspections, and had received
letters saying: 'Get lost, Polak, you're not wanted here,' and

how finally one night his consignment warehouse had been set on fire; he'd had to pay another penalty too when it got out that he'd lodged a complaint with the League of Nations commission.

"So in this frame of mind he got home to Mościce, where a summons to the police was already waiting for him. 'Don't go,' said Grandmother Maria, wringing her hands, 'maybe better go back to Lwów and wait it out there somehow.' 'They can't do anything to me,' said Grandfather, shrugging. 'It's sure to be because I haven't handed over the Mercedes yet. I read the announcement – I'll tell them I was visiting family out east and I'll show them this' – he took out the Red Army requisition receipt. 'After all, they're collaborating, so maybe they'll swap the car to make their statistics tally.' So just imagine," I said, glancing at Miss Ciwle, "Grandfather took that receipt to the police-station with him, but the Gestapo officer who interrogated him wasn't too bothered about it; their problem was that Grandfather hadn't reported for work, thereby boycotting the Arbeitsamt orders. You have to know," I explained, "that the factory didn't just produce fertilisers for farming, but explosives too. Then the Gestapo officer opened a folder containing the suspect's dossier, took out copies of Grandfather's expert reports and patents and threw them on the desk, saying: 'We know all about you and we have a final proposal – from now on you are no longer a Polak but an Austrian of German descent, and tomorrow you'll turn up for work.' That very same day," I concluded my story,

"Grandfather was imprisoned in Tarnów jail, from where they took him to Wiśnicz, where there were already several hundred other such 'undesirables', and from there they all went to Auschwitz and got low, three-figure numbers with the letter P on their uniform triangles." "What if he'd done as your grandmother said?" asked Miss Ciwle anxiously, "what if he had got across to Lwów?" "He'd surely have ended up in the Donbas mines," I said, turning off Błędnik Bridge onto May the Third Street, "like Stefan and Adam Baczewski, who died there in 1940."

My dear Mr Hrabal, I felt very sorry for Miss Ciwle, because instead of spinning more jolly yarns, instead of amusing her, when she was in a far worse state than I was – to put it plainly she'd lost all hope for the future – instead of offering her the handful of anecdotes I still had up my sleeve, I had told a tale of martyrdom, without even knowing how in my version of events those sunny picnics by the River Dunajec, skiing in Truskawiec or hunting the balloon-fox had ended in requisition and a three-figure number for Grandfather Karol, the terrible end of Mr Bronstein's family in a mass death-pit near Buczyna and the no less cruel death of the Baczewskis in the Donbas mineshafts. Yes, I felt guilty as I looked at her sorrowful face, and the moment we turned onto the road through the Ochota Estate allotment gardens, I suddenly realised that not everything in my family history that was connected with Mercedes Daimler-Benz had ended in a funeral march and the bitterness of defeat, but that years later, here in Gdańsk, life had added one more chapter to the story, which couldn't fail to cheer Miss Ciwle up. So I shifted down a gear and said: "You know what, life did in fact turn an extraordinary circle, because one day my father, who was a poor man his whole life in communist Poland, came home a bit late from work, or rather he drove home — "

But my dear Mr Hrabal, that day I couldn't develop this consolation theme, I wasn't able to set a bright, sunny coda to that gloomy score, because, staring into the dark, Miss Ciwle had noticed flames dancing around her wooden shed. It really was a horrific sight – the fire seemed to be reaching higher than the bushes surrounding the hut. "Jesus Christ, step on the gas, Jarek, Jarek!!" she cried, repeating her brother's name, so I stepped on it, the wheels surged forward in the sand at the corner, the back end of the Fiat swung round, and I spurred it on so hard down the final short straight that we finished braking with the nose of the car in the wooden gate. In a single bound Miss Ciwle leaped over its broken palings and reached the shed, ready to jump into the fire, drag Jarek out and save their home, but luckily that wasn't necessary. Once I'd backed the car out and parked it where the fire brigade could drive up close if they needed to, once I'd run after her, I heard her laughing loud. "Physic, why are you always fooling around? I thought it was too late. And as for you, Bootboy, do you always have to put so many twigs on the fire? My heart was in my mouth. Let me introduce you," she said as I came up to the bonfire, where Jarek was sitting in his wheelchair too, tucking into a sausage readily held up for him by Bootboy. "This is my student, and these are our neighbours from the allotments." "We don't grow carrots here," said Physic, shaking my hand, "we live here, like her." "We sometimes drop by with a stolen chicken for the bonfire," joked Bootboy, "to feed Jarek." "I'll go and get some ham and bacon," said Miss Ciwle, moving towards the shed door. "Physic, pull up the grill, it's in its usual place."

And soon after, my dear Mr Hrabal, Physic had fetched a grill from the storage box, while Bootboy had beaten down the fire and added a few fatter logs. Meanwhile I held up the grilled sausage for Jarek to nibble at, smacking his lips and purring with satisfaction; after each small bite I wiped his greasy lips and chin with a handkerchief, but he refused to eat the last bit, giving me a look to say I was to consume it because I must be hungry, so I accepted his gift and patted him on the shoulder, at which he leaned his head forward to touch my hand and stammered out a lengthy "uuu-uuu-uuu", which was supposed to mean "thank you". Meanwhile on the grill set up by Physic Miss Ciwle had put some slices of ham sandwiched between bacon and onion, sprinkled with herbs and moistened with olive oil. Bootboy handed out bottles of Heweliusz beer, while from a little silver box that looked like a miniature sugar-bowl Physic tipped some white powder onto a saucer, took a little glass tube out of his pocket and used it to suck the powder up his nose. Then he passed the tube and saucer to Bootboy, who with great relish, but not in any hurry, did the same, and I shan't hide the fact, my dear Mr Hrabal, that I knew what was coming next; I'm sure I'd have let myself be tempted, if not for Miss Ciwle, who whispered in my ear: "Don't take it, I've got something better for later…" So when Bootboy offered me a snort I politely declined, the little glass tube and the saucer were put away, and we ate slices of roast meat and drank Heweliusz beer chilled in a zinc bathtub, while Physic told the story of his most successful summer in California when he was right at the top, had piles of cash, women loved him, and he gave lots of interviews.

It all started here in Poland, because Physic, I should explain, really was a physicist; he used to work at our local university as a teaching assistant, but his wages were so rotten and he wanted to go to America so much that he started making cement breeze blocks and air bricks here at the allotments. As this was in the final years of the military regime, the goods sold like hot cakes, Physic was soon employing half his faculty in his manufacturing venture, and had plenty of cash for his dream ticket to Chicago and for the start of his American journey. But over there, on the other side of the pond, things didn't go quite so smoothly; he hadn't a blind hope of getting work in his own profession, his cash dwindled rapidly, he tried various jobs, and his visa ran out – in short, he was soon broke. And once he was at the very bottom, spending his nights in the most horrible dives, along came a magical moment, the kind every immigrant dreams of, a surprise gift from fate, a Hollywood-style twist in the plot.

Sleet was drizzling down in Minneapolis as Physic tramped the streets in worn-out trainers; all he could think of was suicide, but before that final solution he wanted to get warm somewhere, so he went into an art gallery, where an exhibition was in the process of being taken down, some sort of installations made of wood, wooden beams with incisions cut into them by a mechanical saw. As Physic was watching the workmen lugging these unwieldy constructions away, a yuppie guy in a tie came up to him and said: "We're closed today, but in three days we'll have a new exhibition. Please don't obstruct our work." So Physic replied: "Leave it out, man, I'm an artist from Europe, I'm not obstructing anyone, I'm just checking out your gallery's potential." "What potential?" asked the guy. "Mobile potential, dummy! You've probably never heard of my sort of art, but then these days America is clutching at straws – once it gave us Pollock, Beuys and Warhol, that was the America we were all brought up on, but nowadays it's just chasing its own tail – the real pulse of art is back in Europe." As he said this, he showily lit a cigarette and walked up and down the large gallery space, completely ignoring the guy; he squinted at the ceiling, counted his paces, and stared through narrowed fingers at the light cast by the halogen reflectors, thinking that any moment now they'd throw him out of the heated interior, where his trainers were still leaving soggy patches on the floor. Pre-empting this painful moment, he headed for the toilet and that, my dear Mr Hrabal, was that, because as he passed the half-open door of the office, he heard the man in the tie yelling down the phone: "You must be crazy, Lee! You're out of your mind! The show's three days away and you're on the booze again! You haven't delivered at all, you don't even answer my calls – I've had it with you!" Evidently the artist said something ugly in reply, because the guy in the tie just said: "Fuck you, Lee!" And that was the end of the conversation. So Physic calmly went to the toilet, washed his face and hands in warm water, then took off his revolting, soaking wet trainers and dirty socks, acrobatically raised first one leg, then the other, put his frozen feet into the washbasin, and let a torrent of warm water gush out. While he was in the middle of cleaning himself up, the guy in the tie came in; their eyes met in the mirror, and before the guy had a moment to say anything, Physic roared at the top of his voice: "I can't fucking stand anyone spying on my rituals!" to which the guy in the tie whispered: "Excuse me," and at once retreated. Physic threw his stinky socks in the bin, wrapped his feet in paper towels and put on his slightly drier trainers, but instead of leaving, he went back to the now empty gallery space and stood in the middle, then walked into each corner, muttering under his breath: "This is no good, it stresses me out, it's too fucking static for words," while the guy in the tie peered round the door at him. Finally Physic came back to the very centre of the room, lay down on his back, folded his hands under his head and stared up at the ceiling. The guy in the tie came up to him and asked: "Can we talk?"

And that was the real turning point; next day Physic's genius shone bright, when in the same trainers, but wearing a new coat, he stepped into the gallery and pressed on its owner an ample portfolio full of quotes from reviews of his exhibitions, pictures of his works and excerpts from theoretical essays, which all combined to form the phenomenon known as "mobile building art", or mobuart for short. Yes, Physic was undoubtedly a genius; who else could have created such a coherent and convincing, though completely fake computer simulation in a single night? It remains a mystery where he managed to get some money, a computer, a scanner, some paper and a printer that night, not to mention all the materials he needed to create the non-existent art of an as yet non-existent artist; suffice it to say that the newspaper headlines in all sorts of languages, the titles of his reviews, and above all the colourful photo posters of his "happenings" delighted the gallery owner. "It's a return to basics," he said with a glint in his eye. "You're like manna from heaven! So what are you gonna show us the day after tomorrow?" At this point Physic laid a cost estimate for the happening on his desk and replied that a true artist never discloses his intentions too early, because his work is spontaneous and revelatory, breaking all the set patterns and conventions. The gallery owner liked that even more, because without batting an eyelid he immediately wrote out a cheque, merely worrying whether or not mobuart would catch on.

But Physic's genius wasn't exhausted yet. Just imagine,

my dear Mr Hrabal, on the day of the exhibition, when numerous critics, yuppies and art experts had gathered for the occasion, there in the empty gallery they saw two cubes, two boxes positioned more or less at the centre of the room; it looked as if some light bamboo frames had been covered in thick, opaque black plastic. But this wasn't a performance by the Bulgarian artist Christo, not just some banal concept to do with interiors and exteriors, as the audience realised as soon as Physic tore the black plastic from the first of the mammoth-sized cubes. Everyone held their breath – yes, it was a concrete mixing plant set up vertically on wooden runners, exactly like the one Physic had had at the allotment on the Ochota Estate. At a height of several metres, at the top of a steel hour-glass there was an intake for sand, cement and water, and at the bottom there was an outlet for the mixture of materials, which by opening a small tap could be released into moulds positioned underneath. And so the creation of art began – the plant was set in motion, while two helpers bustled about with the moulds. Soon after a third assistant rolled a powerful fan heater into the room, to dry the blocks of cement. Meanwhile Physic had opened the second, smaller cube, revealing a man and a woman sitting on wicker chairs: they were both naked, still and silent as they stared into space. Only now, as the first blocks were starting to dry out, did the profound, artistic purpose of the happening become clear: with one of the workmen helping, Physic started building around the couple, erecting four walls with no doors or windows, in order to seal up an as yet invisible cell. My God, how the audience loved it, especially when Physic went up to them, handed out bricklaying trowels to anyone eager to join in, and explained how the cement blocks should be laid to keep them vertical. My dear Mr Hrabal, there were more eager participants than jobs to be done, so they took turns every fifteen minutes. So the walls rose, the mixing plant roared and rumbled away, spitting out more and more building material, while the fan heater dried out the fast-setting cement Physic had so cleverly used; the critics, yuppies and experts took off their jackets, rolled up their shirt sleeves and got covered in lime as they literally vied with one another to do the work, not just laying the blocks but also willingly carrying them from under the mixer to the heater and from the heater to the building site. All this was recorded by cameras from the biggest TV channels, who'd been summoned by an influential critic, who – without consulting the artist, it has to be said – interpreted the happening as a symbol of the Holocaust: unfeeling society walling in a cell where the first man and woman, Adam and Eve, would die in the darkness for lack of oxygen. So by the time the two naked people really had been completely walled up, with a ceiling on top, there were more than fifteen television channels in the Minneapolis gallery and ten radio stations, not to mention sundry photo-journalists and hacks; some had interrupted their broadcasts to go over live for three minutes and report on Physic's happening. Even as it was going on it was already being hailed as the greatest artistic event of the season. Here too Physic proved his genius, because whenever they ran up to him with a camera or a microphone, he roared at the top of his voice: "I've fucking told you, not now, I'm on the inside, right in the middle of space and time, I'm in the process of becoming a human being, so fuck off, this is my birth, wait until I emerge from my foetal fluid!" That sort of remark made the journalists go crazy, the air was thick with superlatives, the tension rising like before a storm. Then Physic started painting the concrete bunker black with an air-brush, saying out loud: "Graffiti is shit, graffiti's over, now you create the mega-literature of symbols." And then the entire company rushed at the freshly bricked-up walls with spray cans handed out by Physic and his helpers; some wrote their initials, others wrote slogans like "Fuck interest rates!", while others made impressions of their hands. Some of the ladies, heedless of the presence of cameras, or quite the reverse, fully aware of them, took off their knickers, coated their buttocks in paint and made bum prints on the concrete sarcophagus, which might seem to prove they'd seen Jiři Menzel's film of your book. Once all four walls were covered in daubs, Physic gave a signal, pickaxes were brought in, and once again with the audience's participation he began to hack a hole in the wall, which the influential critic later called "a gateway to the interior of light, the victory of objectivity, the key to compre-hending the tragedy of the downtrodden". Then each person could lean over the breach in the wall and catch a glimpse of the couple copulating; by now, I should explain, a symphony of sounds was raining down on the entire gallery out of loudspeakers, including storm noises and the rush of water trickling down drains. Meanwhile Adam and Eve were adding to the musical background: with each heave, each copulatory thrust, he let out a loud cry of "Kilimanjaro!", while in a soft, warm alto she ululated in reply, which the influential critic later interpreted in his immortal essay as the transgression of rescued souls from the sphere of the subconscious into the sphere of articulated fantasy, i.e. emancipation from sex, public life and mass death brought by napalm and nuclear weapons.

"Yes, I was at the top in California," continued Physic, snorting another pinch of white powder. "After two years of being constantly on the up, when my mobile building art brought me piles of loot, I was like God, I could do literally anything. My cycles of pyramids, cylinders, three-dimensional rhombuses, saucers, glaciers and galaxies were compared with the works of Leonardo, though that was an exaggeration because Leonardo created practical designs that were impossible to realise, while I realised world-scale ideas in practice, but so what?" said Physic, passing the glass tube and saucer to Bootboy. "If it hadn't been for that sonofabitch Lee, that degenerate piss artist, if it hadn't been for his furious White Anglo-Saxon envy of a vagabond from nowhere, if it hadn't been for his maniacal rage, I'd still be sitting under the palm trees, or zooming down Sunset Boulevard in my Mercedes 300 convertible. I'll be frank about it – it was that

Mercedes of mine that finally made his cup of bitterness overflow – that loser, raving that I stole his thunder in Minneapolis! It was a sports coupe with automatic gears, leather upholstery and air conditioning; when he saw me rolling down the boulevards, really laid back, nice and slow, when he finally realised that all the dirty tricks he'd played on me – dogging me at every step the length and breadth of the USA, like the phone calls to say a bomb had been planted at every single one of my private views – had actually misfired, when he compared his own nonentity with my success and, as I said, saw his enemy, God Number One, driving that Mercedes, the devil got into him, a cold, calculating devil, and for the first time ever he used his head and set the federal dogs on me. It didn't take them much time or effort to find half a kilo of Colombian coke in my car – needless to say, I'd never set eyes on it before. But not even the lawyers could do anything – I didn't have a visa extension and by then I was nothing. My lucky star that rose in Minneapolis had fallen into the Pacific, but no one really noticed; they were bored with mobuart by now, and neo-fluxus had just come into fashion – I can't bring myself to say what a bastard child that is, generated in New York. So I was deported, but the only thing I regret is the Merc – I could have shipped it across and had a bit of cash here at the start, but those scum, they didn't stop at accessing my bank account, they confiscated the car too, citing some paragraph about the instrument of crime, period."

"How many more times is he going to tell this story, I

wonder?" said Bootboy, handing the saucer and glass tube back to Physic. "However many times it takes for you to understand," Physic retorted, "that if you've got enemies, don't buy a Mercedes." "Yes," laughed Miss Ciwle, looking my way, "that's just what we're planning to do!" "All that's nothing," said Bootboy, clapping Physic on the back. "If you'd only seen him when he got back from America, standing in the nettles at the same old allotment, looking at the rusty concrete-mixer and sliding his hand over it. Do you realise, he soon came running over to my place and said: 'Bootboy, let's go back to our roots. How much is cement these days?' So I told him it had all gone down the Swanee and so on, but he refused to believe the door had slammed shut on the spontaneous era of heroic manufacturing, cutting off a few fingers here and there, he refused to believe the steady stream of cash had already changed its course five times over, steering well clear of this neighbourhood – he refused to believe in anything, he got depressed and started drinking. Then he wouldn't emerge from his den, and just threw his leftover bread to the birds. And then, if you please, as he was feeding all those sparrows, wagtails, chaffinches, siskins and thrushes, something changed in that thick skull of his and he finally began to see the light; he remembered a story he'd once read about Saint Francis, in which apparently the great preacher found inspiration in feeding the birds." "Nonsense," interrupted Physic, finishing off a bottle of beer. "He's off now," he explained to us. "Next he'll be telling you I saw the birds change into snakes and spiders, as if I'd had visions in the wilderness, but it wasn't like that." "So what is your shed with weeds up to the ceiling," yelled Bootboy, "if not a wilderness? Even if it's not, it's a hermitage at least. You may not be a martyr, but you're definitely a preacher." "Stop it!" said Physic, interrupting him again. "You see, he's getting it all wrong again." "Hold on a minute," cut in Miss Ciwle unexpectedly. "If you don't stop shouting we'll have to call it a day."

But my dear Mr Hrabal, it wasn't much use; Physic and Bootboy were already so high they'd need a hang-glider to get down again. In fact it didn't bother me at all, especially as a lucid picture of their pioneering enterprise soon emerged out of their jumbled remarks and contradictory arguments. Apparently Physic was the first to hit upon the idea, but it would have been impossible without Bootboy. In short, Physic had installed a computer with the Internet in his shed, and one day he'd been in touch with a curate from a parish in Sucha Górka; the young priest admitted, as frank as could be, that next day he had to give a sermon, but composing anything that made sense, and that his parishioners would find digestible and understandable, was pure agony, because how many times could he fulminate against drunkards, how many times could he expatiate on the sinfulness of divorce? As Bootboy had a top-class degree in Polish studies, Physic suggested he should do the Christian thing and help the man by coming up with a few thoughts. Just for fun Bootboy wrote a lovely little speech for the curate from Sucha Górka, entitled

"Saint Francis wanders in the supermarket", and from then on, my dear Mr Hrabal, they had a new trade. It was a phenomenal success, and before long they had more than forty orders a week flooding in from all over the country, so Physic took care of the logistics, while Bootboy gave up school and hacked out text after text. But the expectations soon exceeded their modest capacity as demand outstripped supply at least four times over. At this point Bootboy proved no less a genius than Physic: from then on they stopped selling standard texts on their website, but offered a variety of rhetorical solutions instead, sections that they put together from the best models. So when a priest from Radom was suspected by his parishioners of excessive conceit, Bootboy took a topic entitled "modesty" from the file and tossed him a ready-made phrase, something in the style of Cicero: "In truth, my dear friends, I am the last person to teach you a lesson, but the present situation obliges me to do so", and so on; when a parish priest from Owczarków was collecting signatures against the new constitution, he could simply click on the menu headed "Argumentatio" and find a classic quote from Father Skarga, to wit "a bad law is worse than the cruellest tyrant", which naturally helped him to prove that the communists were a mere trifle, a picnic, child's play compared with the present Jewish-liberal dictatorship from Wall Street; and when a certain canon was looking for something on Darwin, he was sent Number 33 of Schopenhauer's *38 Ways to Win an Argument*, in the form of a phrase saying "that's all very well in theory, but it won't work in practice". A week later theological issues were added too, and besides the topics you could easily get ready-to-use quotes from Saint Augustine, Pascal, Thomas Aquinas or Cardinal Newman on their website. After about three months the team of students employed by Bootboy had created a unique skeleton framework, a universal preaching code which, with the help of a few access paths, even the most whimsical of priests could use to compile a masterpiece homily of his own free choosing, ranging from something for the ecumenical council right through to the hard-line views of the schismatics.

Yes, my dear Mr Hrabal, I felt relaxed as I listened to it all, because after putting Jarek to bed Miss Ciwle had come back with a ready-rolled and lighted joint; while Physic and Bootboy were arguing about Bishop Jankowski, who had demanded a sermon about his own Mercedes within the week, which was giving them trouble because none of their topics had dealt with anything like that before, while they were wondering whether to get their teeth into the problem from the Divine Providence side, or from the work ethic angle (the most reverend gentleman had not condescended to specify this in his order, but was mainly wanting to preach a counterblast to some easily identifiable secular journalists), while they were bellowing unrepeatable oaths aimed at Bishop Jankowski and his sybaritic lifestyle, to put it as subtly as possible, I breathed in the smoke and felt not just the weariness of the entire day pouring off me, but of all the years

I'd been describing to Miss Ciwle during our nocturnal drive. I could feel my soul becoming fantastically light, my desires pure and innocent, my body weightless and my thoughts airy, when suddenly the garden in Mościce came into view: Grandfather Karol was sitting in a wicker armchair, reading; his summery panama hat cast shade across the upper half of his face. Grandmother Maria was cutting tea roses; flooded in strong sunlight, her whole figure stood out like a bright splash against the stone wall of the orangery. "Is this your fiancée?" asked Grandfather, putting down his book as Miss Ciwle and I approached the terrace. "She's my instructress," I replied timidly, "she's teaching me to drive." "Yes," confirmed Grandmother Maria without looking up from the roses, "in his time that's quite normal." "But have you finished at the polytechnic yet?" asked Grandfather, looking at me intently. "This isn't your son," said Miss Ciwle, smiling, "it's your grandson." "Oh yes, quite so," said Grandfather, not letting her finish. "Quite understandable and...very beautiful." He got up from his chair, came over to Miss Ciwle, took her hand and discreetly examined her profile. "I meant your features – they're unique. Would you please allow me to go and fetch my camera so I might make a portrait?" "How beautifully he spoke to me," whispered Miss Ciwle once he had vanished into the cool interior of the house. "It's a good thing he'll never hear Physic or Bootboy, or he'd draw some hasty conclusions." "Don't tire him too much," said Grandmother Maria, walking past us with a bunch of roses. "He's worn out by his own time, he should stay in the shade," she added, vanishing into the glazed orangery. "Does he really want to take my picture?" asked Miss Ciwle. The sun was at its zenith as the torrid air shimmered above the blanched garden foliage, expressing the sweet fragrance of flowers under the cupolas of a heavenly apple tree and some apricot trees. The heat was making our clothing cling to our bodies, so it felt unbearably confining and heavy, like a beetle's carapace; there we stood on the terrace, immobilised by insect-like lethargy for the whole of eternity, until at last overcoming the resistance of the sun-baked air we slowly entered the house, where total silence reigned. Taciturn porters were carrying boxes and trunks downstairs, and all the rooms, the parlour and the library were in an indescribable chaos of scattered and isolated objects.

"Look at this," I said, picking up a company envelope from Mr Bronstein's shop. "There's something inside." I opened the flap and took out a grey rectangle of Gevaert photographic paper with nothing exposed on it. "Read that, it's my grandfather's handwriting." Miss Ciwle leaned over the card and read in a half-whisper: " 'They took me away to a place where the creatures looked like burning fire, but could assume the appearance of people if they chose to.' " Then she turned it over and read out another sentence he'd written: " 'Next I went to a place where there was nothing.' But you've smoked yourself silly!" She laughed out loud as she tossed some more wood chips on the fire. "No driving for you

... *I picked up a company envelope from Mr Bronstein's shop. ... I opened the flap and took out a grey rectangle of Gevaert photographic paper...*

tomorrow. But anyway I'd like to hear what your father did when he got back from work." "I can't explain now," I said, having trouble getting my tongue to obey and watching every word I uttered fly off on its own, only to collapse in a heap of letters, black flakes that went spinning on the flickering flames of the bonfire, before finally dissolving. "It's a bit strong," I said, handing back the roll-up, "and I did it wrong too." "But I showed you how to do it – slowly and gently," said Miss Ciwle, blowing out smoke. "You're more like a locomotive." But without letting her finish, my dear Mr Hrabal, I confessed my guilt – I admitted picking those weeds in her absence and leaving them to dry on my balcony in the hope of edifying my soul and liberating my body. Instead of getting angry, instead of telling me off, she burst into laughter. "What a funny student you are! And what a bad botanist! These herbs get their strength from purity and virginity," she said, picking a stem and rolling it in her fingers. "What I've got in my hand here is a male specimen, and when it's in bloom it tries to get pollinated…" – she picked another stem – "…by a female sprig like this one, but then the whole effort goes to waste, because pollinated grass hasn't any strength left in it, no magical properties, so while it's flowering you have to uproot all the male specimens" – she pushed one of the stems into the fire – "and then the female stems and flowerheads get swollen with essence as they grow." "Like nuns devoted to God," I blurted out without thinking. "If only you knew," said Miss Ciwle, solemnly knitting her brow, "there's nothing funny about it. The supernatural power of the soul is always derived from renunciation – all the female saints and sorceresses knew that, but nowadays you can't say it out loud." "Are you crazy?" Now it was my turn to laugh out loud. "We're living in a free country." "Free for whom?" she firmly cut me short. "Doctor Elephant? Physic? Bootboy? Or perhaps in some strange way you were thinking of me, as a liberated woman, weren't you? I'll tell you something," she said, dragging deeply on the roll-up, "that first winter when Jarek and I ended up here I almost went off my head – there was no heating, no running water and no toilet, not to mention cash or any sort of job. So I worked as a dancer at the Lida bar, on a pole, on a swing, and in a shower cabin, but I had a deal with the boss: no whoring. Uglymug used to come and watch me every night – he just sat there burning, sweating and moaning, inviting me over, standing me drinks and saying: 'I'll do anything for you.' It went on like that for weeks, until finally I asked: 'Do you really mean anything?' 'Whatever you want,' he drooled, 'whatever you demand.' When I told him, 'All right, a driving instructor's licence and a small Fiat of my own,' he almost fell off his bar stool. For a month I was left in peace, but when he came back again and put a document and some car keys on the bar, it was me who almost fell off the pole. I'll tell you something else too," she said, tossing the stub into the fading fire. "I'd never screwed a guy before, I was a virgin – excuse me, but I was a real young lady of virtue, as they used to say in polite society, including your grandparent's salon, for sure."

My dear Mr Hrabal, I was speechless; meanwhile Miss
Ciwle scattered earth on the embers of the bonfire and added
that the stems I'd dried on the balcony were useless: I'd
picked them too early, and they were bound to be male
anyway. I wanted to say goodbye and thanked her for the
supper, but she said it was out of the question. "Where on
earth are you going in a state like that? You should never
smoke again – you haven't got any tolerance, like me with
alcohol." And she went to fetch a hammock, two blankets and
a pillow from the shed. "I hope you're not afraid of the
company," she said, glancing at the hedge, behind which the
old cemetery lay in silence. "Thank you," I said, "but I'm
going to make my way down the hill to a taxi. There won't be
any driving tomorrow, so let's make a date for the day after." I
set off towards the gate, but my feet slowly began to lose
contact with the ground, as if I were wearing Hermes's winged
sandals instead of shoes. I floated forward a few metres in this
pleasant state of weightlessness, though at an extremely
limited height, and landed on the ground, just like Neil
Armstrong on the moon, childishly amused by the reduction
in gravity. I took another step and floated again like before,
laughing louder and louder, but then suddenly something
strange happened, because instead of being there to meet my
next gentle landing, the ground began to recede from under
my feet, and suddenly I found myself high above the trees, the
hill and the Gothic brick of the Hanseatic city; inside I felt the
sort of incredible lightness and non-existence that plenty of

mystics must have spent their whole lives trying to achieve. Embarrassed at the very idea, I strained to give my body some weight to draw me downwards, but it wasn't easy – my state of suspension must have gone on for quite a time, until finally I heard Miss Ciwle's cry, which, like a shell from Captain Ostoja-Kończypolski's anti-aircraft battery, struck me somewhere near the heart, and at last I fell down – not like the SP-ALP Mościce balloon that flopped onto the meadow near Bobowa, more like a rusty Tupolev with burned-out engines – it was a terrible crash. Afterwards I slowly got up, streaming with water. As she helped me to struggle out of the rainwater barrel Miss Ciwle thundered in a ringing tone: "He who cannot walk shouldn't take up flying. You appear to be one of those people whose bread always lands butter side down. Lucky you didn't fall in the compost." "It's a miracle," I said, tapping on the barrel. "Do you see? This font here has returned me to the community, dressed in new robes" – I wrung out my trouser leg – "and I've gained a new spirit too, I'm fresh as a daisy." "Well, I don't know," she replied, putting the pillow on the hammock. "I must go to bed, I'm getting up in three hours' time." But before closing the shed door she came up to me, my dear Mr Hrabal, gave me her hand in parting and said: "Thank you."

There I stood outside her home in total amazement – what on earth did she have to thank me for? It was I who should be grateful to her for the terrific evening with Bootboy and Physic, the high-speed course in modern art, the know-how of the Prophet Internet service, and finally the lesson in how not to smoke grass when you've never done it before. I walked along the cemetery fence, thinking about it all, and to tell the truth, once again I entered the vale of despondency; a dense fog had arisen over the shipyard and the bay, and from somewhere in the port a navigational siren was wailing. Closer by, an invisible tram was ringing its bell at the junctions. The air was sticky with oppressive dreams failing to reach resolution in redbrick houses, alleyways and gardens. Once again the city was becoming overgrown with nettles, couch grass and pigweed; I'd never liked it – alien, despicable and unreal, every year it sank a millimetre deeper into the rotting stump of its own myths, as if it wasn't getting a large enough dose of sunlight, as if the old smell of herrings, tar, rust, soot and agar were still casting an impenetrable shroud over the greasy water of its canals, the rotten remains of its piers, its socialist blocks and unrestored granaries.

"You're starting the day in a sour mood, Sir." The taxi-driver's essentially friendly face was like all the incarnations of Klaus Kinsky in one. "If you so wish we can get a ration of beer on the way – twenty-four-hour service was *unmöglich* in Jaruzelski's day, Sir, but now it's *möglich*, everything's *möglich*." The clapped-out Mercedes from the generation with fins literally began to fall apart on the corner of Kartuska Street – the wrecked diesel engine spewed out gusts of exhaust, the doors rattled, the shock absorbers thumped, a loose window dropped and the inside was filled with a thick, suffocating cloud of air freshener, the mint-scented variety. "Well, if not, I'll just hop out for some cigarettes," said the driver, revealing his intentions. "You wait here." He stopped outside the all-night shop near the training ground. "Back in a moment," he said, as the door creaked and slammed. "Don't fall asleep now." I watched a small fire burning near the rubbish heap under the chestnut tree, where the dervishes and dossers, the followers of Saint Vitus, the boozers, meths-drinkers, winos and hoboes of both sexes were warming their rags in a glimmering circle. Now and then the image was shrouded in a thickening mist, and my dear Mr Hrabal, their faces, their figures, their slow, sparing movements reminded me of insurgents agonised by a long march, who have dodged the occupying army for a while and are seeking an illusory moment of respite, illusory because the breaking dawn, which they haven't even noticed, will bring them certain death, the rotten, nasty kind.

We set off again in the dreadful Mercedes, the taxi-driver reeled off his monologue, and I sensed that my evening and night-time driving lesson was not yet complete; it had to have a continuation, just as there was another chapter to the story of the 170, not the one stolen by the Soviets – that had a petrol engine – but the one that appeared one spring day in '72 on the corner of Chrzanowski Street in Upper Wrzeszcz at my father's instance – that one had a diesel engine and far greater mileage, which obviously had to be mentioned in the epilogue. "But will Miss Ciwle want to go back to the subject?" I wondered as I paid the taxi-driver. "Will she want to turn another circle in our motoring course?" And just imagine, my dear Mr Hrabal, she did want to – the day after next, as I was walking down Sowiński Street to the Corrado school, she leaned her shapely head out of the window of the little Fiat and said: "Hello, Mr H., you're a quarter of an hour late. Do you men always have to complicate things?" I was flummoxed, because that evening, after the grass, we hadn't actually fixed a specific time to meet, so I kept quiet as I did up my seatbelt and adjusted the mirror. But she was in a really good mood, and as soon as I set off she said: "Today we'll deal with intersections – first let's go to Hucisko Street, and I finally want to hear what your father did. I expect it had something to do with your grandfather's cars." "Of course," I said, turning into Kartuska Street, "but before I tell the story, you ought to know about the background. So" – I stopped at the lights outside the City Council – "life was extremely grey and impoverished. We lived very modestly; indeed, my father was an engineer, but he didn't belong to the modern, vanguard, wholesome class of people. For years on end he earned less than a tractor-driver at a state farm, a shipyard worker, a milkmaid or an unqualified plasterer, but he never complained, he never made a sour face. Even when we had nothing but bread and dripping to eat before his monthly pay day, he used to smile and say: 'We've survived worse than this.' He never indulged in reminiscences about the good old days because he was always sure even better times would come in the end, though to tell the truth" – we were still stuck in a jam outside the City Council – "I never could fathom the source of his noble-minded optimism, which couldn't possibly have come from experience, only from some seam of naïve goodness, buried deep in his soul. Where else could he have got his belief…" – we slowly moved away from the ugliest building in the city – "…that life would get better, when it only got worse and worse?" "Perhaps he believed in God," said Miss Ciwle, giving me an inquiring look. "If someone's got it in them deep down, not just on the surface, even when the lions are eating him he reckons that despite some temporary setbacks, things are basically going in the right direction." "Well, maybe it was something like that," I said, laughing as I braked at the top of the Crab Market, "though his faith in God owed more to the spirit of quantum physics than historical events. But as if life wasn't so bad," I got back to the point, "despite feeling disgusted by the excesses of the progressive, vanguard, wholesome class, despite responding to all their campaigns, rallies, marches and hysterical vocifera-tions with restrained silence, only in one instance did my father ever go against his principles and talk about the past, and that was when the subject of cars came up." "Surely he didn't like Syrenkas and Trabants?" Miss Ciwle cut in. "I didn't put it right," I explained. "The point is that whenever my mother, my brother or I said to my father: 'Oh, how nice it would be to drive to the beach, even in a Syrenka, instead of being squashed into the tram for an hour, how good it would be to come back from Kashubia with baskets full of mushrooms, even in a Trabant, without waiting in the pouring rain for the last bus that's crammed to bursting and flies past the stop without even slowing down,' and whenever we rather timidly mentioned that such-and-such a neighbour had finally bought a Syrenka or had had the luck to win a Wartburg on the lottery, my father would tell us that not every vehicle with a two-stroke engine automatically deserved to be called a car, just as not everyone who speaks from a tribune is purely by that token a statesman, and he would cut off further debate with the statement that if he were ever to drive a car, it would only be the sort his father used to have, so we could moan as much as we liked, because the very idea, the very dream of going to Sopot beach or the Kashubian lakes in a Mercedes belonged to the realm of the phantasmagorical.

"Years went by; Polish Fiats had appeared on the streets by now, you only had to queue once at the delicatessen's to buy two packets of coffee and a tin of pineapple chunks, a few people had brought clapped-out old Volkswagens across from West Berlin, and some of the sailors used to swish along Gdynia's Świętojańska Street in Talbots or Pontiacs, but my father hadn't changed his mind at all. So just imagine," I said, and drove barely five metres forward before getting stuck in the traffic again, "that April afternoon when under the windows of our little flat we heard the typical whirring sound of a finely tuned diesel engine, and a joyful choir of screaming children running after a slowly approaching Mercedes 170 DS chanting: 'It's the Gestapo! It's the Gestapo!' Yes, that was a really great moment for my father, his time had turned an extraordinary circle right before our eyes – a high-pressure fuel injection one-hundred-and-seventy, a post-war vintage, it was almost identical to the old one with the petrol engine. It had the same bulbous mud-guards as in the photos, the same elongated nose with the radiator, and just the same large rear end, all of which gave you the feeling that any minute now Grandfather Karol would step out of it. But instead of him my father appeared and joyfully beckoned us over, inviting us on our first outing along the streets of Wrzeszcz. We drove down Chrzanowski Street, then Polanki, admiring the dashboard and its Bosch dials, the steady purr of the engine and the gentle swaying of the suspension, while my father told us how difficult it had been to find certain missing parts, how he had hunted them down at scrap-yards and old workshops, and how there were parts that couldn't be bought or found anywhere that he had turned on a lathe, because you have to realise," I said, switching off the Fiat's engine, "repairing that Mercedes, which my father bought as a write-off from a mechanic friend of his, took two whole years, and it was all done in secret, because it had to be a big surprise." "Incredible," said Miss Ciwle, lighting a roll-up, "your father must have been a real romantic." "Well, actually, he was an engineer," I replied, starting up the engine to move two metres before stopping again. "Nothing gave him greater pleasure than breaking down. If we went on a long journey to the mountains and nothing happened, nothing broke, my father would drive in silence, plainly bored by the monotony, but as soon as the gearbox started grating, or the brakes started squealing, or the differential gear started knocking, straightaway with a gleam in his eye he would reel off various conjectures, make diagnoses and develop hypotheses, and once we had reached our destination, instead of coming hiking with us, he would unpack his tools and rummage about in the engine from morning to evening, covered in oil stains up to his elbows; he was happy if a few days later when it was time to be getting home, he had finally found a tiny crack in the rubber seal on the brake pump or a broken thread on some screw. That was when the real battle against time and matter would begin, but my father never lost it – the repair was always completed at five to twelve, when we'd set off down the highway home, and the slightly gloomy mood into which my father would now fall for lack of any subsequent breakdown was fully compensated for by the impression that the shape and look of the old Mercedes made on other drivers. Sometimes they flashed their lights at us, sometimes they waved and sounded their horns, but the greatest emotions were stirred by overtaking; a Trabant, for example, or a Zaporozhets would get close to our car, and for a while its driver would keep at a safe distance, surprised that such an old relic could get up to ninety, but suddenly he'd step on the gas, flash his indicator and start overtaking, upon which my father would gently accelerate and at somewhere around a-hundred-and-ten through the left-hand window we'd see the flustered, sweaty face of the Moskvich or Trabant owner, who would literally go goggle-eyed, stick out his tongue and scowl horribly, for our speedometer would already have reached a-hundred-and-twenty-two kilometres an hour, and the Mercedes still wouldn't have had its final word, its engine purring and its suspension gently swaying, so if in the end we were overtaken, my father would smile to himself, stroke the steering wheel and say: 'I mustn't tire the old girl out.' But sometimes the Trabant or Zaporozhets had to take cover behind us when a truck came roaring the opposite way, and then its driver went completely nuts, sat on our tail hooting and flashing his lights, then started his next overtaking manoeuvre without due thought, on a hill or a bend, or heedless of a solid white line, and twice the outcome was serious, though not tragic. The first time a Trabant with Kielce number plates shot off a curve in the highway and crashed into a haystack, and the second time the same thing happened to a Romanian Dacia with Poznań plates, which ended up in a pond. Naturally, my father immediately slowed down and turned around to lend a hand, but his behaviour was clearly not in tune with the etiquette of the era, because the Trabant driver hurled abuse at us, calling us idiots, dicks and swindlers, while the Dacia driver, up to his calves in water, shook his fist and screamed that people from Gdańsk were all criminals: they didn't just block the way for decent people, they still drove scrap metal left by Nazi bigwigs, and what a

pity so few of them were killed in 1970." "Never!" cried Miss
Ciwle. "Didn't your father punch his lights out?!" "He'd have
had to go into the water," I explained, "and secondly, like
every time he had to deal with that sort of rudeness he didn't
fly into a rage, he just felt depressed. 'Don't forget to let the
fish out of your boot,' was what he said to that Poznań upstart,
and I can tell you," I said, finally moving off in first gear, "it was
better than sloshing about in all that mud, because when the
Dacia driver heard the remark about the fish, he was
dumbstruck, went completely purple and got so enraged he
kicked his own car door, then started running violently
towards us, but he fell over, got up and fell again. By the time
we saw him emerging from the pond, up to his ears in slime,
the Mercedes was already carrying us off down the highway,
and as he changed gear my father told me and my brother:
'Now you know why you mustn't overtake on a bend.' "

"What a fine lesson," laughed Miss Ciwle. "I couldn't
have given a better one! Those repairs and breakdowns are
just like in Hrabal's story – wait a minute, which book was it
in? the bit about dismantling the engine..." "*The Little Town
Where Time Stood Still*," I answered like lightning, my dear Mr
Hrabal. "Every time Francin had to find an assistant to hold
the screws." "Exactly," said Miss Ciwle, looking at me keenly.
"Did you do that too?" "No," I said, as we drove at the speed
of a tortoise along a small square, where two powerful cranes
were trying to lift a Soviet tank, a monument to the city's
liberators. "My father had a friend with a garage and a

workshop, but it was in Gdynia, so if he had to take the engine apart or rummage about in the chassis he went there for the whole day and came home to Wrzeszcz on the last train. In time the Mercedes needed more and more frequent repairs, taking two days, or even three, so my father took a sleeping bag and sandwiches with him and spent the night in the workshop, and only once he'd finished the whole job did he come home in the car, tired out, in dirty overalls, smelling of oil. But Mama was not as happy now as the first time he drove into our yard. 'What a sight your hands are!' she'd fret as she served his supper. 'You spend hours on end lying on the concrete floor.' But my father was optimistic, of course. 'We'll soon have the trouble fixed,' he'd reply, 'it's just a matter of patience and we'll come out on top again.' 'Yes,' said Mama, refusing to give in, 'only for you to spend another week with your tools. You could give it a rest, you're tired out, we don't have to have a car at all' – she put her hand on his head – 'you could always sell it to a museum.' 'A German one perhaps?' he asked sarcastically. 'They're sure to have that model already, and in much better condition too, because we Polaks haven't got any spare parts, we're evil, dirty, drunken and idle. Do you know how often I heard that during the war?' 'All right then,' replied Mama, 'you'll do as you wish.' "

At this point, my dear Mr Hrabal, I had to explain to Miss Ciwle that throughout almost the entire occupation my father worked eleven hours a day in a car repair workshop, thanks to which he wasn't deported to the Third Reich as a forced labourer, because the workshop provided services for supply firms and the army. " 'You'll do as you wish,' replied Mama, but she knew perfectly well he wouldn't give up the Mercedes, because that car meant more to him than just an ordinary car, or even an ordinary Mercedes," I continued, reaching the Hucisko roundabout at last. "When finally the cost of an hour's driving began to be about thirty-nine hours in the workshop, Mama got upset and said: 'I'm never getting in that old rattletrap again.' And she never did; one day when the starter wouldn't work for the umpteenth time my father slammed the door, hid the keys in the sideboard, left the car standing by our garden fence and never touched it again." "So what happened next?" asked Miss Ciwle. "Couldn't they make it up?" "No," I went on, "because each of them was rigid with anger, and in their own way each of them was right. Meanwhile the Mercedes rotted away in the heat, rain, snow and frost, and over the next two years it got overgrown with weeds like a steamship on a dried-up river bed; the nettles, couch grass and pigweed were almost up to the roof, thieves had smashed the windscreen and removed the dashboard with the Bosch dials, cats had pissed on the seats, children had ripped off the mirrors, badges and hubcaps, and what was left was finished off by rust and damp, until finally…" "Sorry, please turn around here," interrupted Miss Ciwle. "It's impossible to drive normally in this city any more – it's taken us a whole hour to go less than a kilometre."

So I turned back at the Hucisko roundabout, by the

building that once housed the commission of the former League of Nations in what used to be the Free City of Danzig, but it wasn't as easy as all that: the lights weren't working, so the traffic was being controlled by two young policemen who couldn't cope with the torrent of vehicles, the mechanised mire that was surging forward from all directions – trams clanging, trucks hooting, and cars shuffling along like snails in the torrid heat of the last day in May. Suddenly I realised that this was the final circle I would turn in Miss Ciwle's little Fiat. "If only we had the metro here," she was saying, "or a separate lane for trams, or at least some bike paths. What on earth do they do all day?" She cast a glance at the dismal megalith of the City Council. "I really don't know, but if anything they used to be interested in wrecked cars," I said, getting back to the point, "because once the Mercedes had spent a third year by the fence, covered in wild vines, like a huge dragonfly with empty eye sockets where the headlamps used to be, an official from the Department of Aesthetics knocked on our door and ordered us to get rid of that hideous wreck, as he so graciously put it, because the sight of it was having a bad effect on local well-being. And that was the end," I added, finally turning from Hucisko back into New Gardens Street, "of the Mercedes era in our family, the final curtain, as they say; the car ended up at the scrapyard, where it sat among the locomotives, cranes, scaffolding, water tanks and train tracks waiting its turn for the giant crusher. That day my father put away his driving licence and never talked to anyone about cars again."

"He finally capitulated," said Miss Ciwle. "I can understand how he felt, but those few years must have been like a holiday for him." "Of course," I replied, "I never saw him so happy and animated, either before or after. Those were his sunniest days, a real festival, compensation for all the lost years and deception, because you have to know," I said, managing to cross into the middle lane, "that the first few years after the war were very hard for him. Grandfather Karol was one of the so-called 'enemies of the people' – as soon as the war ended he reported to the factory, but was told it would have been better for him to have died in Auschwitz, because bourgeois engineers weren't needed now, retrograde science was rapidly being liquidated, and when he asked the secretary what was bourgeois about his research and patents, he was arrested for provocation. And so his life had turned an extraordinary circle, because when he finally came out of prison they wouldn't let him live in Mościce, and he could only go and see Grandmother Maria there three times a month, with a special permit for every visit. To bring this sad theme to a close, I'll tell you that after the war my father settled in Gdańsk and studied at the polytechnic here, but whenever he had to fill in a form giving personal details the box marked 'Origin' caused him a lot of worry and insomnia, because he always wrote down 'intelligentsia' rather than 'bourgeois', which was to a large extent true, but it would only take one little report by some Party hothead for him to be accused of hushing up the facts, which in those days was a serious matter. So he used to have sleepless nights, getting very upset in case someone denounced him for having an enemy of the people in his family, that 'bourgeois engineer in liquidation'." "It's just like Hrabal," laughed Miss Ciwle, "except that he was a writer 'in liquidation', while your grandfather was a defunct chemical engineer." "Yes, that's an interesting comparison," I said, stopping the little Fiat at the top of the Crab Market again, "bearing in mind the uncanny continuity of all that sharp practice, because you see, when General Jaruzelski rolled the tanks out onto the streets I was a callow young journalist..." "Let me guess," said Miss Ciwle, without letting me finish, "your workplace was liquidated." "Exactly," I said, and we were both laughing now, "and I never went back to my profession."

Just then our conversation was interrupted, and I never had time to tell her how greatly that final 'liquidation' had influenced my entire life, how much I owed to Generals Baryła, Żyto and Oliwa – thanks to them I had a typewriter I'd taken from the Solidarity building, and thanks to them, instead of running off to press conferences, writing press releases or watching Lech Wałęsa make mincemeat of his rival, Andrzej Gwiazda, thanks to those generals, instead of editing telegrams and telexes I was able to write my first book, which, fortunately, no one actually wanted to publish, but which is still lying in a drawer to this day, my dear Mr Hrabal, as an occasional reminder of those happy days, that first big holiday of ours, that freedom festival when we were so nobly intoxicated by a wind from the sea, which was followed, not all that rapidly, by the inevitable quagmire of politics, the anguish of commonplace things, the poetry of scandal, the epic of deceit, the festival of infamy, in short, normal life with its credits and debits. But I didn't tell Miss Ciwle all that at the Crab Market, where the two enormous cranes were now lifting the Soviet T-34 tank, because some old soldiers from the People's Army, the Civic Militia, the Voluntary Reserves and probably several dozen other related companies were protesting their outrage and trying to prevent the liquidation of the monument, by waving placards reading "Be Grateful to Our Liberators!", "Don't Falsify History!" and "Dignity and Truth", climbing onto the caterpillar platform so the crane operators couldn't load the tank, lying down there, shouting, singing old battle songs, and unbuttoning their prison-camp uniforms like exhibitionists. The police intervention was rather dozy and compliant, as if those grizzled old gents were performing a "Feel Sorry for the Red Army" happening. It really did look funny – by the time a few portly old boys had been dragged off the platform and the crane drivers had been given the signal to do their duty, the next lot had already clambered onto the caterpillar, pretty slowly and clumsily. Meanwhile the car drivers stuck in the jam were pressing their horns one after another, providing an extraordinary commentary, an incredible racket, like at a football match, though it was hard to tell whose side those motorised fans were on, what they loathed or loved about the show, because as you know all too well, my dear Mr Hrabal, in my rebellious country, whose capital city was razed to the ground, just as in your land of compromise, whose capital city is among the seven wonders of the world, in both these cases and places the vast majority of people did not belong to the professional class in liquidation, because they never drove a wonderful BMW like your stepfather Francin, or sat at the wheel of a Mercedes like my grandfather, never owned shares in a brewery or a chemicals factory – in short, they didn't necessarily feel too bad within the mythical lair of revolution, at mass meetings, rallies and parades. Watching those pitiful veterans as they were finally herded into a corner of the square, I thought of Pascal's statement about inequality, where he says that it's crucial and inevitable, but that as soon as we all rationally agree to it, at once we have exploitation on a scale the world has never seen before. Maybe that's the very reason why those dinosaurs saw that Soviet tank, responsible for levelling everyone and everything, not so much as a symbol of their lost authority, as of a utopia they still believed in, and maybe that's why so many of the horns honking on the Crab Market were voicing ambiguous, undecided views.

"They must be nuts," remarked Miss Ciwle. "Those tanks burned our entire city down!" "It wasn't ours yet then," I replied, "but you're right, those tanks were still running riot in the City Centre, as well as in Wrzeszcz and Sopot, several days after the Germans surrendered. They used them to drive into courtyards, shops and churches, and when there was

nothing left to pillage, they fired shrapnel, then improved on
that with incendiary bombs. There were chases too, that songs
were written about: it was right here, by the Radunia Canal,
that Lieutenant Zubov caught sight of beautiful Greta,
immediately changed course and accelerated. Having no other
way out, Greta jumped into the river; but it was March, after
the thaw when the water was high, so she was carried away by
the current and disappeared in the dull grey eddies.
Meanwhile Lieutenant Zubov had driven his tank into the
canal, but when he saw his booty slipping away, he turned his
warriors out of the vehicle and ordered them to wade up to
their waists in the stream in search of the girl, while he spun
the turret round and out of sheer rancour rained shells to left
and right from that T-34 of his – that's how the façade of the
Hotel Vanselow was ruined, several neighbouring tenements
too, not to mention some beautiful houses with loggias on the
edge of the Irrgarten. As it couldn't get out of there,
Lieutenant Zubov's tank was only dragged out of the Radunia
in 1946 and set up on this spot as a monument to show
gratitude to the Red Army, though things would have been
very different" – we finally moved away from the viaduct – "if
the Germans had won the war in the end and recaptured
Danzig, in autumn 1945, let's say. In that case there wouldn't
be a Soviet tank here, but a statue of beautiful Greta cast in
bronze with the inscription 'I chose death rather than
dishonour', or something like that in grand German style;
every year in March an orchestra would play Wagner here, and

the girls would ceremonially swear they'd sooner perish in the waters of the Radunia like beautiful Greta than surrender their German hymens to the *Untermensch*, even during their temporary victory." "What a smooth talker you are!" laughed Miss Ciwle. "That's just like the legendary Princess Wanda who refused to marry the German prince. By the way," she added, as we were passing the City Council again, "he who sows the wind shall reap a storm." And there we left it, my dear Mr Hrabal, because the traffic jam had finally dissolved; now we were moving rapidly up Kartuska Street, as our final driving lesson came towards its end.

And as is the case in life whenever we expect some sort of a punchline, a coda, some sort of loop to close the circle, no such thing occurs. So there we stood outside the Corrado office, Miss Ciwle leaning on the door of the Fiat while I did the same, but on the other side, as she treated me to a last roll-up, in which I could taste a hint of grass mixed into the regular tobacco. "Thank you very much," I said, "those were really fantastic lessons." "Watch your indicators, and don't forget some of the examiner's instructions are deliberately designed to mislead you," she said, exhaling. "Wrong way turns are their favourite trap." "Yes," I said, "I'll look at the signs. Once I've passed my test, may I come and see your brother?" "Jarek?" she said in surprise. "Yes, Jarek," I repeated, "I might root out those old photographs – I'm sure he'd like them very much. You know, I've got a brother too, who hasn't actually been quite so unlucky, but who's been in a wheelchair for a couple of years now. He's got multiple sclerosis, and he can't really get out the house because he lives in a block on the third floor and there's no lift, so he's always glad of a visit." "Yes," she said, "of course, please drop by whenever you like. I thought in your life, in your world there weren't any things like that, so difficult, and…" she hesitated, "thankless." "Well, why should I tell you about them?" I said, finishing the roll-up. "Everyone's got more than their fair share." "Well, goodbye then," she said, giving me her hand. "Don't go overtaking on corners, especially when there's a Mercedes-Benz in front of your little Fiat." And that, my dear Mr Hrabal, was the end.

I walked down Sowiński Street to the bus stop, while Miss Ciwle was settling her new lady student behind the steering wheel. The woman's loud laughter went on ringing in my ears for a while, as she started telling how she and her husband had just moved here from Germany – she'd never imagined you could take your driving test in a car like this; back home in Germany it'd be out of the question, not just for lessons but for any sort of driving. Finally the roar of Kartuska Street drowned out her incessant twittering; I saw the little Fiat once again from the bus stop, turning towards the training ground, but I didn't want to think about the tramps under the chestnut tree, the slalom made of rubber posts or Instructor Uglymug any more. I was exhausted by the heat, the traffic jam on Hucisko, my own memories, the Soviet tank and this monstrously congested city, which seemed to be losing its breath and what was left of its dubious charms, and suddenly I felt terribly jealous, my dear Mr Hrabal, of those driving lessons of yours on the Java motorbike, because you and your instructor had gone gliding through all the finest places on earth: I began to think of Kampa, Mala Strana, Hradčany, the Old Town, Josefov and Vinohrady, those wonderful pub and beer-cellar gardens, so shady in the summer, and the Secession-era architecture competing with the classical and the baroque at almost every step of the way. Hard on their heels came images of Lwów and Wilno, which were taken by the Soviets and had now returned to the Ukrainians and the Lithuanians as their rightful owners, and although I hadn't the slightest jot of patriotic phobia about it, somehow I felt regret, because the cities we got in exchange were completely ruined, burned to the ground like Gdańsk and Wrocław, violated and abused, while Lwów and Wilno, though agonised by the Soviet occupation and the squalor and pock-marks of communism, were still intact; I could compare their new lease of life to a patient who recovers his strength and former beauty after a bout of typhoid, whereas Gdańsk and Wrocław needed to have limbs amputated, heart, kidney and liver transplants and false teeth fitted, as well as long-term therapy for a broken spine – which, though gradually pieced together, could never guarantee a truly happy life.

I boarded the bus, and on the way to Ujeścisko I resolved not to think about it any more, to break free of all the history involving the Mercedes, burned-down cities, expulsions and

professions in liquidation. I preferred to think about Miss
Ciwle, her profile, the look in her eyes, the fragrance of her
hair, the timbre of her voice, and suddenly I realised that
although I had only parted from her a short while ago I
couldn't remember the colour of her eyes and I'd forgotten
what perfume she wore. Yes, my dear Mr Hrabal, suddenly I
realised that for the past few weeks as I'd learned to drive
Miss Ciwle had been like a beautiful face encountered in the
metro, where in a few short minutes we cast our eyes on
hundreds of people, but only remember one or two, and at the
time we think to ourselves, "Who is that beautiful stranger?
I'd give so much to talk to her for just a moment – no, I'll
never forget her brows and her delicate, almond-shaped
eyelids," but as soon as we get off the train, once we're
rushing down the street, caught up in the whirl of life again,
that meeting of glances in the carriage, fleeting and furtive,
is already in the distant past, a couple of seconds that
flashed by, arresting a wonderful image like the shutter of an
old camera, but only in order to store it deep down in our
subconscious memory. Sometimes this flash suddenly comes
back to us years later, because of some chance association,
sound or smell, and then we write a poem, or lose ourselves
in thought, but not about that particular face any more,
which we can't actually recreate precisely, but about time
and its extraordinary workings that rule our dreams and
imagination.

So it was in this case too, my dear Mr Hrabal – Miss Ciwle

suddenly came back to me, out of the blue, in a completely different time and place, though it was at your instance. Yes, it was on that dreadful day in February 1997, when for the first and only time in its history the television news came up to standard without imitating CNN or any of the commercial channels, when it behaved as a decent Central European channel should, by making its first item the news of your flight from the fifth floor at Bulovka Hospital, your leap into the abyss – your death, my dear Mr Hrabal. At the time I was sitting in The Irishman with my friends; outside on the main road through Wrzeszcz sleet was drizzling down, and we were discussing this and that, when suddenly that news silenced all conversation. "He leaned out of the window of the orthopaedics ward while feeding the pigeons and fell into the courtyard from the fifth floor." It sounded like a pronounce-ment, and we all understood that right now, and only now, it was the end of an era – marked not by the velvet revolution, the fall of the Berlin wall or the victory of Solidarity, not by Desert Storm, or the shot fired at Sarajevo, but by that flight of yours, that coda, that punchline, that extraordinary circle that you had spent your entire life turning, by writing all those books that had done more than any others to help us survive the very worst years – they had consoled us selflessly, given us inspiration and wiped away our tears. At once we ordered some beer and the usual gathering turned into a wake, an ancient ritual to call up the spirits, and there among us stood Uncle Pepin, your stepfather Francin, your beautiful mother,

crazy Vladimir, your Pipsi, all your cats in Kersko, and all your
fascinations and fantasies; and you were there among us, like
the illustrious tzaddik of Bobowa amid the most faithful
Hassidim. We knew every line of yours almost by heart, we
could mull over each quotation at length, relishing the sound
of it, its wisdom and its light. And that's just what we did at
The Irishman, my dear Mr Hrabal, as you were lying in the
cold store, waiting for the doctor's certificate and for your
turn at the Prague crematorium. Each of us shouted out a
quote in turn, while the rest tried to guess if it was from *Too
Loud a Solitude*, or perhaps from *Closely Observed Trains*, or *I
Served the King of England*, and whoever guessed first won a
prize – we all stood him an extra round, but if anyone jumped
in with a wrong answer, he had to stand everyone else a
round. The waitress kept bringing endless mugs of Guinness,
Żywiec and John Bull over to our table, her tray of shot glasses
filled with Beherovka kept going to and fro between the bar
and our vociferous group, and it occurred to me, my dear Mr
Hrabal, that maybe this was the best possible award for a
writer, the most wonderful recompense he could have – here
in a city he never knew, a thousand kilometres north of
Prague, on the main street, that was once called Hauptallee,
then Hindenburg, then Adolf Hitler, then Rokossowski, and
was now called Grunwaldzka Avenue, some middle-aged guys
were swapping extracts from his books, arguing over every
comma and calling each other idiots if one of them made a
cardinal error, confusing, let's say, *Bambini di Praga* and *The*

House I Don't Want to Live in Any More. So I said out loud that you'd probably be pleased with this sort of award, and a proper storm blew up, because it reminded us that it was you who should have got the Nobel prize, not Jaroslav Seifert. None of us actually had anything against Jaroslav Seifert, in fact many of us admired his lyrics inspired by the atmosphere of Prague, but there are dozens of poets of the same class as Jaroslav Seifert in the Czech Republic, Europe and the world, while there are no prose writers like Bohumil Hrabal except for himself, not a single one, we roared, one after the other, as if a representative of the Nobel Academy were sitting with us at our table. "So what do you imagine? Why worry if the candidate will make a good impression during the waltz with the Swedish queen, if he'll make a fluent speech, drink too many glasses of champagne or, God forbid, tip the champagne into a vase and demand ordinary Pilsner? How can you be so afraid of a few indecent words, for example, or His Royal Highness getting a pat on the coat tails? When Bill Clinton came to Prague he did so purely in order to drink a beer with Bohumil Hrabal at the Golden Tiger, because American Budweiser is like piss compared with the Staropramen there, and someone like John Irving, he may have written ten successive volumes of *The Water-Method Man* and made a Hollywood serial out of it, but that didn't mean he couldn't offer Bohumil Hrabal a glass of beer. Do you really imagine, you Swedish slow-worms, that a man like François Mitterand went to Prague just to see Jan Hus's monument, or was it to tell

Bohumil Hrabal: 'Ever since I've read your books I don't have to drink Vichy water any more'? Gentlemen of the Academy, how could you fail to notice that Bohumil Hrabal was the most modern, avant-garde prose writer of the twentieth century, while having nothing to do with the avant-garde barbarians, that venal rabble who, apart from copying a few gags off Cabaret Voltaire from Zurich, haven't a clue how to cobble anything together! But from the most meagre shreds, scraps of sentences, leftover bits of images, wallpaper, photos, sounds and odours Bohumil Hrabal made unique phrases, amazing constructions, fairytale worlds and stories; those vibrant words of his always echoed with the elegance of Mozart, the force of Beethoven and the melancholy of Chopin. What do you imagine, you under-educated bumpkins, who on earth had the same magician's ability to pick up some ordinary thing from the rubbish heap of our history, our wonderful civilisation, and turn a scrap of old newspaper into a page in a Great Book, a page burning with his own, not any reflected splendour?" But my dear Mr Hrabal, the Swedish academicians wouldn't dream of listening to us, so we told Agnieszka to bring us some paper, an envelope and some stamps, and started writing a letter to Stockholm, in which we insisted categorically that the Nobel prize be awarded to you posthumously, my dear Mr Hrabal, that they frame the diploma in quartz and place it on your grave at Kersko, where all your cats are sure to be playing in the sun. I had to play the role of secretary, which wasn't easy, because they all kept shouting in my ear in turns: "Have you put this?" "Did you remember that?" "Add that as Poles we've never been so unanimous."

As I was leaning over the table, writing down all their demands, suddenly out of the corner of my eye I noticed a familiar face on the television screen. There, smiling at me from the political news in brief, was none other than Instructor Uglymug. Of course he wasn't wearing a sweaty polo shirt any more, he was no longer a driving instructor and probably didn't swear, at least not in sound and vision. From the scraps of sentences I could hear I worked out that he was a high-up official responsible for ownership changes, and was eagerly privatising everything still left unprivatised, battling to reshape the terribly backward Polish economy, and I can truly say, my dear Mr Hrabal, that the brief report didn't rattle me at all, I didn't find it at all strange – quite the opposite in fact; it was simply the crowning moment for the slogan of the political party that Uglymug had tried to recruit me into. But a whole sackful of information was being spilled on our television news that day, because a few minutes later, as I was handing the letter to all my friends to sign, then to completely random people too, who also wanted to make their contribution to awarding you the Nobel prize, as I was going round the entire pub, gathering more and more signatures, Physic and Bootboy appeared on the television screen with their faces blurred, for the accused are entitled to this right. There I stood under the screen, completely dumbstruck – yes, it was them, without the shadow of a doubt, the biggest hackers in independent Poland; the prosecutor was just reading out the indictment, which was awash with complex paragraphs, but the essence of the case was clear. The combination of Physic's Internet genius and Bootboy's prophetic gift had produced a result beyond all expectation – there was no company, bank, post office or military base they weren't capable of breaking into; they had got the better of the gateway to the Pentagon, the codes of Brussels and the ciphers of banks, and had made themselves quite at home, finding good merchandise everywhere. No, my dear Mr Hrabal, they hadn't stolen money from anyone's bank accounts – they had sought confidential information and sold it for a high price. The Bank of Switzerland could obtain all the details of their rival Asian firms from them, the Russians could get the latest star wars plans, the Americans could get the plan for Yeltsin's favourite game, the Palestinians could get documents from the Israeli Mossad, Mossad could get the addresses of Arab terrorists, a Colombian drugs cartel could get lists of FBI agents, Citroën could get Mercedes' latest designs, Mercedes could get Toyota's, and Toyota Citroën's. The lawyer announced that the case was without precedent and would end in acquittal, because none of the injured parties had brought any formal charges, only a complaint about the activities of a company registered in the Bahamas, Physic & Boot Corporation, whose legal and fiscal competence did not come under Polish jurisdiction, although the owners were Poles. In short, my dear Mr Hrabal, I stood there goggle-eyed, as they say, for to make something like that out of a sermon-writing firm, to sail down an electronic river onto such big oceans from an allotment shed, was no mean achievement for the lads from the Ochota Estate, and even if it wasn't all legal and above board, they had managed to make my city famous, the way Benia Krik, the gangster king, did for Odessa. The camera showed Physic and Bootboy's two-room office on the top floor of a new tower block, then panned down to the parking lot, where there were two identical, silvery Mercedes cars, and that was the end of the bulletin.

I sat at the table and handed my friends the letter to the Nobel Academy. They started reading it carefully, but I was past all that by now, so I quietly drank a Beherovka, then a beer, then another Beherovka, and thought of nothing but you, my dear Mr Hrabal, and Miss Ciwle: where might she be now, the girl who gave her brother your books to read? Was she watching television, or maybe she'd heard about your death on the radio? She was sure to be upset, and was surely thinking, just as I was, about the darkness you had passed into; throughout your life it was no stranger to you, it tempted you many times – at any rate, when you saw Franz Kafka on the balcony of the Kinsky Palace, staring downwards and hesitating whether to jump or not, what you said about the terror he felt was actually about yourself. Yes, I think Miss Ciwle and I understood each other without speaking – she knew that your bitter melancholy, that ultimate knowledge of

nothingness, was the main theme of your laughter, jokes and
irony, not just an escape; she knew that all the tankards of
beer you drank in the pubs and all the stories you wrote were
just a means of survival, an eternal Sisyphean task, a response
to infamy, a way of filling in the black hole, and as she reached
for the grass she must have felt she was in a similar situation:
one more step and the gangway would break loose. Surely just
like you she didn't believe in Ahura Mazda, builder of a bridge
to the other side, which souls cross over to pass into eternity,
and if we were talking about you now, I thought, about your
jump and flight from the fifth floor of Bulovka Hospital, I'd be
sure to bring up the twelfth tablet of Gilgamesh, featuring the
lament of the spirit of Enkidu, summoned from the
underground – those terrifying words, how his body was full
of weeping, and just like an old rag the worms were eating
away at him, like an old rag; if Homer had known those words,
the lament of the ghost of Achilles to the living Odysseus
would have taken on a different, more pitiless form. If we'd
ever had a glimpse of what Orpheus saw, not in song, a hymn
or other religious solace, but in that actual moment of very
present danger, out of sheer terror we might never again be
able to write a letter, drink a cup of tea, make love, eat, or even
die, my dear Mr Hrabal. If I were sitting with Miss Ciwle now,
I thought, here at The Irishman, or at her place, in the
allotment shed, if we were conducting this funeral service
together, this requiem mass, instead of writing a letter to the
Swedish academy, instead of outshouting each other across

the beer-soaked table, we'd surely have been silent, slowly smoking some grass, and that would have been our prayer for you, our tribute to someone who, as he walked that narrow gangway, aware of the imminent finale, smiled calmly, waved his hand and sang in endless praise of summer, as if not wanting to put his loved ones off existence or investigation – for one day someone might succeed in discovering what Gilgamesh never found. And so, my dear Mr Hrabal, you were wiser than all the modern philosophers, who don't know what it's like, so they scream and tear their robes apart, whereas you knew, but instead of behaving like them, instead of wittering on about deconstruction or synthesis, you wrote those beautiful, long sentences of yours, tied like ribbons around the sacred tree of the dervishes. Miss Ciwle and I would surely have exchanged these few quiet words about it, then nicely stoned, we'd have got into her little Fiat with a few of your books and gone to the training ground under the chestnut tree, where each night there's a bonfire, and we'd have hung your volumes on the sacred tree like votive offerings; the bad, dirty and detestable or normal, unfortunate people there would have stared at us as if we were angels, who had floated down from heaven and hung tablets with magic pronouncements on the branches. That would have been the most wonderful way to commemorate your death, my dear Mr Hrabal – I thought, as I drank up the last Beherovka – the perfect finale.

I left the table and went out into that dreadful February

night, walked down Grunwaldzka Avenue and turned into Sobótki Street, where I'd lived for a couple of years since splitting up with Anula. I went upstairs to the loft to dig out from the desk drawer those photographs I'd found during that last move from Ujeścisko. Once I'd done it, I called a taxi and told the driver to take me up the hill, where the allotments lay; there I waded ankle-deep in soggy slush, but instead of trees and wooden huts I saw a sleeping building site surrounded by a fence made of raw planks, on which a yellow board announced that this estate would be called Olympus. The dug-out pits and foundations gave some idea of the future shape of the houses, whose walls would be sure to shoot up in the spring, but there was nothing for me here. I felt as if time had turned another extraordinary circle, and I tried to translate that into Czech, so the first sentence of the letter I decided to write to you would sound familiar; when I got home and sat at the table, I spread out the small set of photographs from Chaskiel Bronstein's company envelope, and that first sentence rolled out all by itself, and you already know it – *Milý pane Bohušku, a tak zase život udělal mimořádnou smyčku* – I sat in total silence, in no hurry to go anywhere.